CHARLIE'S ASHES

A Greatest Generation Story

CHARLIE'S ASHES

A Greatest Generation Story

Richard Barlow Adams

Charlie's Ashes
A Greatest Generation Story
By Richard Barlow Adams

This book was originated in the United States of America.

Other Books by Richard Barlow Adams:

The Parting: A Story of West Point on the Eve of the Civil War

Eben Kruge: How "A Christmas Carol" Came to be Written, also on Audible

Sông Bé: The Dream (Anticipated launch, June 2023)

DEDICATION

To the "Greatest Generation" and those of the same mettle.

FOREW0RD

I joined an august group of wizened veterans in Destin, Florida, in 2020. The group calls themselves the Crispy Warriors, and they represent all the Armed Services, meeting for breakfast once a week in a very hospitable *Crackings* restaurant. We are about 70 in number and represent pay grades E-4 to O-8. Almost all of us are veterans, retirees, or both. There is wonderful fellowship and there are wide ranging discussions of our experiences in uniform, the state of the nation and our respective services ….and great jokes.

During my first visit, I learned that their name originated many years ago when there were but few of them and they ordered their bacon crispy.

I only had the privilege of meeting two of the group's "greatest generation" members featured in Rich Adams' novel *Charlie's Ashes*, Sam Lombardo (101) and Joe Gossen (96)—the others being John Beard (102), Bill McCowen (93), and Charlie Geiger (93). They were clearly a special breed and warmly lauded by Governor Mike Huckabee, himself an honorary Crispy Warrior, during a standing-room-only breakfast, November 2, 2017.

I can attest that those I did know were sharp as tacks, humble, and loved to laugh. But I had not a clue how heroic their service to the nation was until I read *Charlie's Ashes*.

Rich Adams, himself a Crispy Warrior, is a West Point graduate, a Vietnam veteran, and an award-winning novelist. Not to preview too much of his story, the WWII veterans take the stage at a Crispy Warrior breakfast, as they live rather pastoral lives in an assisted living facility. From there, Adams frames a tension-packed story with jaw-dropping flashbacks based on interviews he conducted with each of the veterans about their experiences in WWII.

I look forward to future encounters with these mature combat veterans and to learn more about their exploits and contributions to the nation.

Philip A. Dur, Rear Admiral, USN, Author *Between Land and Sea*

"Old soldiers never die. They just fade away."

General Douglas MacArthur
Addressing a Joint Session of Congress
Washington D.C., April 19, 1951

James Montgomery Flagg Poster, popularized in WWI and WWII.

PREFACE

We Americans live in a nation conceived "under God." It survives on the sacrifices of professional, volunteer, and drafted men and women who for nearly two and a half centuries have defended our freedoms and our constitution. Such men and women, unless in uniform or highlighted on the Fourth of July, Memorial Day, or Veterans Day, or disfigured, or fitted with prosthetics, are often indistinguishable from the rest of society—their patriotism, heroism, and emotional scars unseen. *Charlie's Ashes* is their story.

Richard Barlow Adams

CHAPTER ONE

November 1, 2019, just blocks from the crystal-clear emerald waters of the Gulf of Mexico in an eatery called Crackings in Destin, Florida, Sam Lombardo, a century old and an infantry platoon leader in France and Germany during World War II, scanned the faces of friends seated around four-top tables linked together to form a thirty-foot table in the restaurant's back room. He relished the thought of another glorious morning with like-minded men, mostly sixty years and older and wearing the same white embroidered short-sleeve shirt.

"Now that, John—that was a good one," Lombardo said, complimenting John Beard on an unexpected punchline.

Lombardo spotted Rachel, the waitress who mothered the weekly group. In her mid-twenties, she was tall, attractive, and had perfect white teeth.

Finished with the orders, Rachel whisked through the main dining room to the kitchen.

Lombardo sat at the end of the table, Beard on his left. Beard, six months his senior, was a B-25 bomber pilot during WWII. Next to Beard, Bill McCowen, ninety-three, had been an aircraft gunner. Next to McCowen, Ron Webb, eighty-three and nicknamed Igor, ejected over North Vietnam on his 53rd combat mission. Joe Gossen, on the other side of Lombardo, was ninety-four years old and a ball-turret gunner in the belly of a B-17 bomber. The seat next to Gossen was empty, and on the other side of the empty seat sat Murray Casey, a mid-'50s retired Navy Master Chief Seal who, despite entreaties, resisted giving details about his nine Seal Team deployments in the Persian Gulf and Afghanistan.

Tommy McCraney, dubbed TM, African American and a Vietnam veteran, entered the room and ambled up to the empty seat. "No Charlie today?"

"Apparently not." McCowen pulled out the chair. "Have a seat."

"Always an honor to sit with you oldies," the 73-year-old Marine said.

McCraney turned to Casey. "You too, kid."

Casey obliged McCraney with an elbow.

"Who's calling who a kid?" Webb quipped. "How old were you in Vietnam?"

"Enlisted in late '67," McCraney said. "Got to Vietnam in June of '68. So, nineteen. You a POW then?"

"From '67 to '73," Webb said. "So, yeah. With five years to go."

McCraney shook his head. "Unbelievable, I mean, freakin ... unbelievable." He turned to Casey. "Had you been born earlier, you and your Seal buddies could have slipped in and gotten Igor out."

Lombardo caught the grin on Webb's face and cleared his throat. "Looks like it's my turn, and this one you might not remember."

******

In the kitchen, Tommy Green, the eatery's owner, beamed. "Got yourself another good crowd, Rach."

"Yeah, I do." Rachel blew a renegade wisp of highlighted brown hair from her eyes. "Thirty-eight so far, and record time getting their orders. But then, I know what most of them want."

Greene chuckled. "Bacon."

"Yep."

On the other side of the glass wall that separated the main dining room from the back room, a man and a woman eyed the veterans group.

The man, in his sixties, sported an LSU 2019 National Football Championship T-shirt, shorts, and flip flops. He shook his head. "I don't know, Fran. They're all wearing the same shirt. Maybe some sort of club?"

Cloaked in a flowery coverup, the woman sipped her coffee. "Beats me, Herb."

When Rachel appeared from the kitchen, the man gestured for her attention.

Rachel approached the table. "Morning, sir. May I help you?"

The man pointed to the back room. "In there. Those men. What goes?"

Rachel smiled. "First time with us?"

"Yeah, me and the wife are from Louisiana. Breaux Bridge."

"They're mostly former military, sir. They breakfast here every Thursday morning. Have been for years. They're sort of a big deal around here."

"What's with the shirts?"

"They call themselves the Crispy Warriors because most of them like their bacon crispy. It's on their shirts, along with their names and the service insignias. You know—Army, Navy, Air Force, Marines, and Coast Guard. The newer shirts have the Space Force."

"Then veterans?"

"Yep, most of them. But not all."

The wife pursed her lips. "Looks like they've been around a while."

Rachel smiled. "Yeah, most of them. Five fought in World War II. Two are over a hundred."

The woman blinked.

"That's right, ma'am. In that room are privates and generals and everything in between. A super bunch of guys."

The man noticed the men in the room suddenly holding hands and bowing. One stood up and prayed. After the prayer, the other men stood up, all of them facing an American flag in a corner of the room. Each crossed his heart or saluted.

"The pledge," the man murmured.

"Yes, sir." Rachel gestured with her coffee pot. "I best be getting in there."

The couple watched Rachel banter with the men and top off coffee cups. The woman slid her hand across the table and patted a faded tattoo on her husband's arm. "That could be you in there, Herb."

In the backroom, Lombardo, his face stoic, delivered the punchline to a joke that had Beard, McCowen, Gossen, McCraney, Webb, and Casey in stitches.

"Damn, Sam," Beard managed after catching his breath. "The rest of us need to hear that one."

"Not around Rachel," McCowen said, unaware she was right behind him.

Rachel leaned over. "It's all right, Bill. I heard what Sam said. And nothing you guys say shocks me anymore."

After Rachel moved down the table, Gossen turned to Lombardo. "How do you remember all those jokes?"

"What blows my mind," interjected McCraney, "is your delivery. Perfect timing, Sam. Always perfect."

Lombardo grinned. "If you told the same jokes as many times as I have, you'd probably have it down too."

Rachel departed and soon returned with another pot of coffee. "Anyone for a hit?"

"Sure, darlin," Lombardo said. "How's my favorite girl?"

"Never better, Sam. And just like every week, folks out there are asking about you guys." Rachel caught the Louisiana couple looking and waved. The man waved back.

Lombardo grinned. "You're the best, Rachel. How long you been putting up with us?"

"Nearly seven years, Sam. Started before I got married. Remember?"

"I do," piped Beard. "And now you got, what ... two kids?"

"Three, John. All boys, and I want full credit."

Lombardo chortled. "Three kids and still the prettiest girl in Destin. You really are a catch, Rachel."

Rachel blew him a kiss.

When she was gone, Gossen shook his head. "You're a dirty old man, Sam."

"Not dirty, Joe. Just a man. Is it my fault I've outlived two wives and see girls as ... you know, girls? It's a God thing. He put it in me."

McCowen rolled his eyes. "Yeah. But he also gave you a brain. You've got her by seventy years."

Westy Westenbarger, the group moderator, with more than 150 combat missions in Southeast Asia flying F-4s armed with smart bombs, stood up and clinked his water glass.

"Heard from the Emerald Grand yesterday, guys. We are still on for Veterans Day, the *Red, White, and Blue Celebration* at HarborWalk

Village. We're to assemble at the amphitheater by 5:00 pm, everyone in white shirts and khaki pants. Same drill as for John Beard and for Bill McCowen's record number of combat missions. We're to enter through the side entrance where they'll have parking blocked off for us. They're really pumped we're coming." Westenbarger glanced at the end of the table. "They're also going to honor Igor for his time as a POW and our WWII vets for still breathing."

Westenbarger shot a thumbs up to the end of the table.

Rachel returned with a tray of breakfast platters and passed them out like a Vegas dealer.

Soon, everyone was into breakfast.

Beard, who only drank coffee in the morning, rose to his feet and clinked his water glass. "Anyone want to hear one of my poems ... again?"

The response was unanimous.

He ambled around the table to the middle of the room, time enough for Rachel to return with another pot of coffee.

Knowing what was coming, she set the pot down and leaned against the glass wall behind Beard.

McCowen winked at Gossen. "Is it fit for mixed company?"

"Mostly," Beard said.

Expressionless, Rachel crossed her arms.

"It's my poem entitled *Captain Dix*. You know, the one I wrote ... hell, I don't remember. Maybe fifty years ago? You've heard it before."

"And want to hear it again!" shouted a Crispy.

"My favorite, John," shouted another.

Beard hiked up his trousers and rubbed his chin as if needing to recall the words, then grinned impishly.

"Few words can say it all, my friends, but as you will later see,
The phrase that says it best, I think, is, "You've gotta be sh*tting me."
Whether said by a soldier or sailor or one of the boys that soar,
Whether said in Europe or Asia or during our Civil War.
No, I believe it goes back a bit further, and the time I've finally fixed.
T'was said by a lass that was peddling ass in the winter of 'Seventy-Six.
George Washington crossed the great river. The storm was a terrible fright.
His men, cold and wet, needed shelter; needed somewhere to weather the night.
The first house they saw was too small, and one was all it could do.
George asked the owner who answered, "Can Captain Dix spend the night with you?"
This Dix was the one who'd be famous, or so the history books say,
For a fort that was named in his honor in a place up New Jersey way.

Beard paused, the impish grin returning.

"Now the next house they saw was quite roomy, and outside a little red light.
Unbeknownst to the clean-cut GW, t'was the home to the 'ladies of night.'
George rapped on the door, and a lady appeared, and to him was a beautiful sight.
George tilted his hat and humbly asked, 'Might you put us all up for the night?'
'I think we can handle the lot of you,' said the lady while counting her tricks.
George said with a smile, 'I've one 100 men—no—make that 99 men without Dix.'
The woman blinked twice, caught full off her guard, uncertain of what she should say,
As the General stood in the glow of her lamp, and she in her red negligee.
'Now, George,' said the lady, her tone so demure, 'I'm a patriot and love that I'm free.'
'But 99 men without dicks, George—"

On cue, Rachel slipped in front of Beard, "—you've got to be kidding me!"

It was a full minute before the laughter in the room died down. Rachel hugged Beard, kissed his forehead, and topped off more coffee cups.

In the hum of the conversations, Lombardo was into another joke when he suddenly flinched, the cell phone in his pocket vibrating.

"Pardon me, guys." He pressed the phone to his ear. "This is Sam."

McCowen saw the color drain from Lombardo's face as he pocketed the phone. "You okay, Sam?"

Lombardo shook his head and glanced at Beard who was talking to Gossen. He rose to his feet and clinked his water glass.

When the room quieted, he cleared his throat. "I've got some sad news, guys. Charlie Geiger died this morning."

Rachel gasped, covering her mouth.

"Yeah," Lombardo said. "Ole Charlie would have been ninety-four next month."

He raised his glass. "A toast to Charlie."

Glasses and coffee cups were raised around the table.

"To Charlie," Lombardo said. "To another dear friend who's passed over the horizon. God bless you, Charlie. We'll all miss you."

Lombardo cleared his throat again.

"We all knew that Charlie was having a hard time of it. He and I talked about what was going on, he and I being so close. Most of you know he was in my platoon in the Battle of the Bulge. A regular GI dogface, but there was no finer soldier than Charlie Geiger. Dependable. He never squawked at what had to be done. Though when he got the frostbite so bad at the Bulge, I had to pack him back to the rear. He didn't want to go."

Lombardo glanced at Beard, McCowen, and Gossen.

"Like all of us, Charlie loved being here. Loved being close to the beach, walking the sugar-white sand. And he loved to fish. Yeah, he did. And it didn't matter if he caught anything. He just wanted a line in the water. But most of all, Charlie loved being one of us, a Crispy Warrior ... one of the old farts. And he told me that when his time came, if it was possible, he'd like his ashes spread over the Gulf."

Lombardo paused.

"So ... what do you think? Can we do that for Charlie?"

CHAPTER TWO

Half an hour later, Lombardo, Beard, McCowen, and Gossen trailed out of Crackings headed for the Patriot House shuttle bus. McCowen, the tallest by four inches, walked slightly stooped with a cane and slow.

In the restaurant, the couple that had engaged Rachel earlier approached her at the register.

"How was your breakfast?"

The man's eyes gleamed. "Young lady, this has been the most meaningful morning I can remember. I can't tell you how special."

His wife echoed the same and handed Rachel a fifty-dollar bill.

"That's so kind of you. Let me get your change."

"No, you don't, young lady," the wife said stiffly. "The rest is yours."

"But ma'am, that's way too much."

The wife pressed her hands prayerfully against her lips. "Young lady, just being here ... seeing those men, how they bonded, knowing what they've been through ... it just meant so much to us, especially to Herb. And don't think for a moment I didn't know you were the only one serving them. How do you manage it?"

Rachel blushed. "Well, thank you, ma'am. I appreciate that."

"And those guys at the end of the table," the man said, "I expect the WWII guys. Amazing how they still have their stuff together."

"Amen to that, sir. Which I suppose is why we're not speaking German or Japanese."

Twenty-five minutes later, the shuttle stopped beneath the covered entrance to the Patriot House Senior Living Facility in Fort

Walton Beach. Beard, McCowen, and Gossen got off, followed by Lombardo, who stopped and turned back to the driver.

"Scotty, how long you been schlepping us around?"

"Be four years this September, Sam."

"This thing run on gas or diesel?"

"Just regular gas. But drinks a lot of it. Gets—I don't know—maybe ten miles a gallon."

"Much to driving it?"

"Nope. These new shuttles are a breeze."

Lombardo entered Patriot House, his home since turning ninety-six. He approached a comely middle-aged woman at the front desk, a pair of horn-rimmed glasses low on her nose.

"Hey, Veronica."

"Hey, Sam," the day manager said, as she sifted through a stack of mail.

Scotty hung the shuttle keys on the wall hook behind her.

"Anything special going on?" Lombardo asked.

"Nope, not really, Sam. Samo-oh, samo-oh Thursday routine." Veronica looked up. "Heard about Charlie, Sam. I'm so sorry. We all are. You two were tight."

"Yeah."

She handed him a flier. "Mind pinning this up on the bulletin board?"

Lombardo read the flier. Printed at the top in large-block red font, *IMPORTANT*. Below, in smaller black font, *Internet will be out of service 9 p.m. tonight to 7 a.m. in the morning.*

"We're switching to another provider," Veronica said.

Lombardo nodded and after pinning the notice on the bulletin board entered the spacious first-floor atrium, open to the fifth-floor ceiling. It served as the home's gathering space, living area, activities center, game room, and group exercise room. In one corner, a snack bar with plastic tables and chairs was set up within a lattice-rimmed arboretum of artificial shrubbery and flowers.

He took a slow spin around the room and offered greetings to the usual suspects, chatting up a few. As he did, the thought struck him that everyone was doing or not doing what they always did or didn't do—that it was the same for him. Each day a carbon copy of the one before, a blueprint for the next.

For the better part of his first year at what he and others called *the home*, he regretted moving, thinking he could have stayed in his two-story apartment another year, maybe two, retaining his freedom and privacy. But Geiger, Beard, McCowen, and Gossen, not to mention the Patriot House marketing team, would have none of it. Regardless, he realized soon enough that he was wrong. Legs that used to leap tall buildings were now slow getting up a staircase. Climbing more than a few required a rest. The home made sense. It would be his last stop.

A shell of a woman waved from across the atrium.

Lombardo approached the woman who greeted him with a warm smile. "Morning, Edith," he said in a loud voice, seeing she forgot her hearing aids again.

Two years his junior, Edith Hebert had been Miss California a year before the big war and had, like himself, outlived two spouses. This and more in common, they were each other's closest confidant. She loved his accent, still thick after ninety years in the states. He was her Italian stallion, and she often called him Dino. After only a few weeks, she allowed him into her guarded life, showed him her old albums, photographs no one else at the home had seen—shiny black and whites defining a much younger and sensually beautiful woman. Personally, he favored the pageant pics, especially the swimsuits. Modest by modern standards, she filled out a swimsuit better than any of the pinup girls.

"Dino, today Crispy Warrior Day?" Edith asked.

"Every Thursday, Edith."

The matriarch of twenty-seven offspring, Edith Hebert was dressed as she always was—to the nines. In a beige linen jacket and pant suit, her face was made up to cover soft wrinkles, her silver-white hair meticulously coiffed. She held court nightly over a gaggle of geriatric girls, the unquestioned grand dame of the home.

A redoubtable raconteur, especially after a few chardonnays, she related life stories, of which she had many, including touring the troops during the war and of escaping Hollywood after six months of mindless modeling to become an executive secretary, eventually marrying the boss and birthing babies. Though, to Lombardo's chagrin, he thought her starting to skip a beat. Her stories, all reruns, were one thing, but in the past month he found her repeating the same story in the same night ... or at least thought he did.

Glancing suspiciously around the room, Edith gestured with an arthritic finger.

Lombardo bent over to give Edith his ear.

"Dino ... the country? Is it safe?"

Her words were slightly slurred.

"Because if it isn't, you Crispies got guns, don't you?"

Lombardo managed a straight face. "For a fact, Edith. And don't you worry yourself. I've got your back."

Relieved, Edith was about to smile but caught herself. She'd forgotten her dentures again.

Moving on, Lombardo walked the wide hallway skirting the atrium to his one-bedroom flat. Opening the door, he flipped on a light switch.

Down a short hallway, the flat opened on the right to a small combination kitchenette-dining nook. Straight ahead, the living room featured two floral-draped windows, a sleeper sofa, side tables, Oriental lamps, a large intricately woven Arabian rug, two Queen Anne chairs, a Cherry wood coffee table, and some Japanese artwork. The pillowed sofa and chairs faced a large flat-screen television mounted over an electric fireplace.

To the left of the living room, accessed by a short hallway, his bedroom included a standard double bed, flanked by small nightstands and smaller lamps. Opposite the bed, a Cherry wood dresser was topped by a dozen small, framed photographs of family. Above the photographs, a shadow box contained his military awards, decorations, various unit insignias, jump wings, and the silver oak leaves of a lieutenant colonel. A small brass crucifix hung above the headboard, and above it, a rendering of Jesus and the holy mother.

Left of the entry hall, a utility closet boasted a washer and dryer and wire storage racks. Beyond the closet a small bathroom featured a handicap shower with bench.

Various other artforms and memorabilia adorned every wall of the flat. Left of the television, a large canvas photo reproduction featured him arm-in-arm with Arnold Palmer on a golf course. Across the sky an endorsement read, *To Sam, a dear friend, an incredible patriot, and a man who can putt,* signed, *Arnold Palmer.*

Lombardo opened the refrigerator, retrieved a pitcher of tea, and poured a glass. He plucked two mint leaves from a potted plant, rolled them between his thumb and forefinger, squeezed them, and dropped them in the tea.

He sat at a small dining room table that faced a wall of framed photographs and sipped the tea while munching a handful of walnuts—what he told people was the secret to long life.

He focused on a photograph taken in the late 1920s in Caraffa, Italy, his birthplace, a village in the region of Calabria at the base of the Italian boot. Ten years old, he stood with his mother and two sisters just months before they boarded an ocean liner to join his father already in Altoona, Pennsylvania. He remembered too well leaving a homeland under the iron hand and boot of Mussolini and his Black Shirts. The Atlantic crossing had been rocky. Arriving at Ellis Island, he and the family became United States citizens a week before the stock market crash of 1929.

His eyes shifted to other photographs. Photographs of his growing up in America, the family expanding by two sisters, him going to school, playing sports, learning the stone mason trade from his father, and graduating from high school to join the National Guard on the eve of World War II. He lingered on a photograph of his graduation from Officer Candidate School, a second lieutenant with paratrooper wings. In a photograph taken with his $48 Kodak 35 Range Finder camera, he stood on the over-crowded deck of a troop ship that took him to war as a replacement in the European Theater just weeks before the Battle of the Bulge. He had wanted in the fight earlier but had been held back for his map reading skills and ability to teach.

Another photograph captured his retirement from the Army in 1966. He was seated with his first wife, behind them a daughter, Michele, and a son, Mark, who later distinguished himself as a Marine pilot, flying helicopters in Vietnam and later becoming a key player in the founding and early years of Federal Express.

Sipping the last of his tea, he eyed a photograph taken at a winery. Smiling and holding a glass of red wine, his arm around his second wife, his children in the background were fully grown.

His eyes settled on a photograph taken at a 100th birthday party at the Pensacola Country Club thrown by his children. Wearing a vintage World War II "pinks and greens" uniform, family, friends, and members of the Crispy Warriors surround him. It had been quite a party. His older sister had flown in from Italy, and throughout the party, a closed-looped slideshow chronicled his life. A lot of people said nice things about him.

He rose and ambled to the bathroom, took a shower, and brushed his teeth, the mirror again testifying to a birthday suit way out of warranty.

CHAPTER THREE

That afternoon, Lombardo strolled by a group of what he called *homies* doing chair aerobics in the atrium, following to the extent they could the lead of a cute, curvy late-teen black girl in colorful tights. The girl tossed Lombardo a come-hither look.

"Come on, Sam, join us."

Lombardo grinned. "Not me, Caitlyn. That's for old people."

Outside, Lombardo breathed deep the sun-warmed fall air, the sky clear, windless. His nose caught the scent of roses as he sat in one of the four lounge chairs surrounding a gurgling three-tiered fountain. The other chairs were occupied by two men and a woman, all napping under sunglasses, arms across their chests.

Beneath the brim of a ball cap embossed with *WWII Veteran* and sporting half a dozen military pins, Lombardo scanned the Northwest Florida Daily News, settling on the sports section.

After a few minutes, Lombardo sensed a presence and lowered the newspaper.

A freckled-faced imp in red shorts and a white top boasting an Eiffel Tower applique stood two feet from his nose.

The little girl clutched a small red rubber ball and a small brown paper sack. Lombardo stared at her, expecting her to blink. But she didn't.

He glanced about for an adult or anyone who might be looking for her. Seeing no one, he folded the newspaper and leaned forward.

"Are you lost, young lady? Looking for your parents?"

"They're inside with my grandpapa," she said, still not blinking and still studying his face. "I'm five. How old are you?"

Lombardo smothered a grin. "Well, I'm pretty old. I'm one hundred years old, young lady. And soon I'll be a hundred and one. How old is your grandpapa?"

"Oh, he's older than that. He's like ... eighty-seven."

"Ahh, yes. That really is old."

"Do you think you'll live that long?" the little girl asked.

"I might," Lombardo said. "If I take care of myself."

Momentarily lost in thought, the little girl wriggled her nose. "Do people come here to die?"

The question caught Lombardo off guard. "Well ... do you know that eventually everybody does?"

The little girl nodded assertively, as if she did.

"Okay. Well, the folks here, most of them, have pretty much lived out their lives. So, I guess I would have to say, yes."

The little girl considered his answer and cocked her head. "Do they go straight to heaven?"

Lombardo marveled at the child's easiness with the subject, especially with a stranger. "That's a very good question, young lady." He rubbed his chin. "And, yes, I believe most people do just that."

"Then I'm very glad to know it." The little girl glanced over her shoulder. "Because my grandpapa ... he's not doing so good."

"Then, I'm very sorry to know it."

"Yeah. He just, sort of ... sits there." The little girl's eyes dropped. "He used to be so much fun. He'd ride me on his back and play tea party. He'd pretend to bite off my nose and ears ... and we played—"

Mid-sentence, she smiled and thrust the ball that she was clutching in front of Lombardo's nose, causing him to retreat a few inches.

"Can you play Jacks?" she asked expectantly, emptying her sack on the pavement.

Lombardo grinned broadly. "If you show me how."

******

At supper, Lombardo sat with Beard and Gossen at a four-top table in the Patriot House dining room where a hundred and thirty meals, more if there were guests, were served three times a day. Beard's wife, Gwen, was in Pensacola with grandkids, and Gossen's wife, Johanna, was dining with her bridge partners. The room resonated with the usual chatter and clinking of silverware and glasses.

"Bill had his supper brought up again." Gossen said as he spooled his spaghetti.

"That's what? The third time this week?" Lombardo mused, regarding the widowed friend.

"Yeah. Not like him to miss eating with us. It's his legs. Playing all those sports growing up, he says his knees and hips are shot. Using a cane most of the time, he doesn't want people to see it ... doesn't want people feeling sorry for him."

Beard sliced a meatball. "So, ole Charlie's going to be cooked?"

15

Lombardo shot Beard a look and sipped wine served from a 1.5-liter bottle. "Got an email from his son. Says we can expect the obituary tomorrow or the next day."

"And his ashes?" Gossen asked.

"Don't know. The family has to agree."

Finishing their meal, a dining room attendant approached with a dessert cart. "Gentlemen, tonight we have key lime pie, warm banana-nut bread, and everybody's favorite, vanilla ice cream. Any takers?"

Lombardo and Gossen opted for the banana-nut bread, Gossen with a scoop of ice cream.

Lombardo eyed Beard sipping his decaf coffee. "You need to beef up, John. Come a big wind, we'll lose you forever."

Finished with his dessert, Lombardo leaned back in his chair. His hands behind his head, he studied Gossen, then Beard.

Beard put down his cup. "What, Sam?"

"Just wondering. Why we keep doing this? Day after day."

Beard narrowed his eyes. "Doing what?"

"The same thing ... every day."

"You going to eat that roll, Sam?" Gossen asked.

Lombardo handed Gossen his dinner roll.

"That's what I mean. We wake up, we eat breakfast. After breakfast, we mill around until lunch. After lunch, we take a nap and wait for dinner. Same thing every day."

"What's the big deal?" Gossen said, mumbling through a mouthful of banana nut bread. "The chow's great."

******

After supper, Lombardo migrated to the atrium and read a posted flier about a Randall Burgess, Ph.D., who was to lecture Sunday afternoon on roses and why they come in different colors.

He spotted Edith and four other women sitting beneath a Kincaid Painting that featured a cottage by the ocean on a rock promontory, rimmed by lush, flowered greenery and nestled beneath a setting sun. Light radiated warmth from a bay window as an ocean wave crashed on jagged rocks.

Approaching within a few feet of Edith who was holding court, Lombardo pretended to read a flier promoting Captain Nemo's Deep-Sea Fishing Adventures.

"I tell you, girls, it's like another country." Edith's tone was dismissive. "Kids today have no idea how we got here, about our history, how the country works. They've got no sense of what it takes to make a nation or to be one. Not at all like us. Remember World War II? All the sacrifices we made, our menfolk. All that and so much more lost on today's generation."

The other ladies listened, each with a stemmed plastic wine glass.

Lombardo smiled. Edith's enunciation was perfect.

"My little Maggy," Edith continued. "She's my youngest great-grand. A fourth grader, she is, in California. You won't believe what's happening there. I asked her if they say the Pledge of Allegiance in school. Ladies, you're not going to believe it. She had no idea what I was talking about."

The others expressed indignation.

"They don't teach it or say it in school, and they don't pray to God in the mornings. I don't know if they're even allowed to say, God."

Edith paused for a generous sip of Chardonnay and daintily patted her lips with a paper cocktail napkin.

"You know how it was, girls. For me, during the war, except when I was on the road, I was in California. All us girls busting our derrieres, me in a ball-bearing factory. Broke every fingernail ... thought I'd never get the grease out. But I couldn't have been prouder. I did my part. We all did. Just like our brave men. Especially, those who didn't come back—God bless them all. And California was the proudest state in the nation. What a noble time. All of us doing what we could."

Edith's eyes sparkled.

"Back then, American flags flew all over California, because the Japs were on our side of the country and we had all those military bases."

As Edith soliloquized, one of the ladies ceased nodding.

"But now ... I just don't understand it, what's happened. And it's all so sad. And such a shame. And worse, the good people of California, and there are lots of them, have no say. They have to stomach all the foolishness that goes on there."

Edith paused for another nip of Chardonnay.

"But God knows all, doesn't he? He knows what's going on. And I know he has a plan for California." Edith's eyes narrowed. "I just wish he might be a little quicker with it. Anyway, thank God, Maggie's family is selling the house and moving to Nashville."

Lombardo eyed the nonresponsive lady, a petite Asian woman.

The Asian woman raised a crooked finger.

"Yes, Wendy," Edith said.

"About World War II, Edith. I, too, know how it was. At least for me." The woman's tone was polite, serene. "I, too, was in California. As a Japanese American, I spent the war in an internment camp. I was imprisoned, Edith. Do you remember that?"

Edith exchanged glances with the other ladies as the Asian woman straightened herself, her shoulders back.

"After Roosevelt signed his executive order, soldiers came to my house. My family was sent to the Tule Lake internment camp in northern California. Tule Lake was one of ten camps we Japanese Americans were sent to. More than a hundred and twenty thousand of us. All of us American citizens, Edith.

"Tule Lake housed eighteen thousand. And you don't want to know what it was like. The barbed wire, the guard towers. All we could take to camp was what we could carry. We were loyal Americans, Edith. We lost our homes and everything else. And why? Because we looked like the enemy."

Lombardo stared at the woman, her eyes moist. He remembered the camps and knew she spoke truth. After the war, the Army sent him to the Defense Language School in Monterey, California, to learn Japanese, then to Japan as part of the occupation force. He knew all about Roosevelt's executive order and the treatment of Japanese Americans during the war.

"I was just a child, Edith," the Asian woman managed after collecting herself. "But I remember it like it was yesterday. My brother, Daniel joined the Army just to get out of camp."

The words seem to stick in her throat.

"Daniel fought with the 442nd Regimental Combat Team, an all-Japanese American unit, except for white officers. They fought first in Italy, then in France and Germany."

A tear trickled down her cheek. Edith grasped her hand.

"The 442 was the most decorated regiment in American history, and almost no one knows it. They received twenty-one Medals of Honor, the highest decoration our country can give. They suffered so grievously ... so much to prove. So many casualties."

Her lips quivered.

"Daniel was killed in France in the Battle for the Lost Battalion. He wasn't even nineteen."

"Oh, my God, Wendy. Oh, my God. I am so sorry. I had no idea. Please ... you must forgive me."

Lombardo was well aware of the 442nd Regimental Combat Team's heroism.

The Asian wiped her eyes with a cocktail napkin.

"Wendy," Edith said, "your Daniel was every bit an American patriot. A true patriot. No different than any of the boys. And the camps—yes, I knew they existed, but I didn't know anything about them. All I remember is that ... people were afraid."

The Asian woman smiled weakly. "Not afraid, Edith. They just didn't trust us."

CHAPTER FOUR

Returning to his apartment after supper, Lombardo poured a 2008 vintage Saint Emilion Bordeaux into a Riedel wine glass. He had decanted the wine before supper, hoping for the best. It was the last of a twelve-bottle shipment that had proved a conundrum—some amazing, some not. He tilted the glass and inspected the fruit. A consistent dark purplish red, the legs thick and slow to recede. He swirled the glass, releasing the bouquet, and poked his nose inside. The aromas teased his nose. Swirling and sniffing a second time, he filled his mouth, swished the wine, and swallowed, savoring it, and smiling. Eye, nose, and mouth agreed. It hadn't turned.

He poured more wine into his glass, sat on the sofa, and sipped. Still perfect. Or nearly so. But something was different. Something was off. The finish? He smacked his lips and ran his tongue across his teeth as if erasing a blackboard. He took another sip, and then a third. Each time, he sensed the same thing. Something was different. Off. Not way off, but off enough that he questioned himself. *Was it the wine or was it him? Were the taste buds the first to go? Were they the first to die?*

He gazed at a framed black and white photograph, cracked and creased, on the coffee table. In the photograph, thirteen American soldiers, including himself, encircled an American flag, the flag handmade and completed on just one side. Most of the men were sitting or on one knee, each with an M-1 rifle. In blue ink across the sky were words he had penned more than seventy-five years ago. *First American Flag on German Soil.*

He lifted his glass. "Here's to you, Charlie. You were still in the hospital. So, you missed all the fun we had with the flag. Greet the brothers up there where there's no frostbite."

He continued staring at the photograph and sipping his wine. The men around the flag were part of his platoon. Helmets off, most were smiling. Two months earlier, they had fought to exhaustion in the Battle of the Bulge, suffering their share of casualties.

In the photograph, they had just crossed the Remagen bridge into Germany, the first Allied division on German soil. A month earlier, higher headquarters had denied him a request for a regulation American flag. Something about no flags being issued to front-line troops. How did that make sense? From time immemorial, men carried flags and banners into battle. They died to keep them from touching the ground.

Incensed, he had vowed to do something about it and told the platoon they would make their own. And they did, piece by piece from scraps of red, white, and blue fabrics collected as they advanced on Germany. It was soon finished on both sides, the flag now displayed in the Infantry Museum at Fort Benning, Georgia.

Indelible in his mind were memories that preceded the crossing of the bridge—the hunger, the bitter cold, half the platoon suffering frostbite or trench foot, or both. The paradox of fear and death versus immortality, that somehow he was bulletproof. All carried a letter in their breast pocket in case they didn't make it. He eyed the four men in the photograph circled in blue ink long ago, the ones who didn't make it. He raised his glass and whispered, "Greater love hath no man."

He drained his glass, reached for the decanter, and refilled it, settling back on the sofa.

Picking up the remote, he tuned to a cable news station.

A panel of three suits prattled on, the talking heads saying what they were paid to say—playing their parts, delivering narratives, and defending and attacking issues. And always in character, always predictable.

What to believe?

He switched to another news channel, one with a differing bent and soon smiled sardonically as a woman—sharp, good-looking, confident— rebutted what the man just before her said, his remarks seemingly unassailable. He noted that her rebuttal never addressed what the man said. But that was par, right? The more unassailable or egregious the points proffered, the less on-point the rebuttal. And no one seemed to care. It was how you played the game. The result often being two or three unrelated premises being pitched at the same time.

What had happened to the Walter Cronkites of the sixties and seventies—the straight shooters. When news was news, and facts were facts, and Op-eds were for newspapers. Now, if someone lobbed a bombshell, the target wouldn't even duck. They'd flick it aside as an annoyance and lob their own. *It was like grade school. If a kid didn't have a real answer, he'd just say, oh, yeah!*

He killed the television and filled his glass with the last of the Bordeaux and revisited what had been playing around in his head since breakfast.

Reaching for his cell phone, he placed a call.

Beard answered. "What's up?"

"John, it's Sam."

"Yeah, I know. It's on the phone."

"Tell me, John ... seriously. Why are we still alive?"

Beard didn't answer.

"I mean, you're a hundred and one, and I'm a hundred."

"So ...?"

"So, why? What's the purpose?"

"Listen, Sam. You're taking Charlie way too hard. He had a good life. Hell, he had a great life. But at the end, he was dealing with a lot of crap. You know that. And we'll all miss him. I miss him. But soon enough they'll be saying the same thing about us. We'll be gone ... and people will miss us."

Lombardo was silent for a few seconds. "I've been thinking, John."

"Oh ...?"

"You trust me, don't you?"

"Trust you? If you haven't gone nuts."

"I haven't. So, hear me out. We need to do something."

"Do what?"

"I want you to meet me out back of the home at five in the morning. Khaki pants and your Crispy Warrior shirt. Don't let anyone know. And don't let anyone see you."

Beard didn't respond.

"John?"

"Yeah, I'm here…"

"Tomorrow, five in the morning."

"That's the middle of the night, Sam."

"Just be there."

"Can I ask why?"

"Nope. And you don't need to know. We'll be back for supper. And don't tell Gwen."

"She won't be back for three days."

Lombardo hung up and called Gossen and gave him the same spiel.

"You in the sauce, Sam?" Gossen asked.

"Don't be a puss, Joe. Beard's in. Five in the morning."

Next, he called McCowen and threw down the same gauntlet.

"I don't know, Sam …" McCowen said.

"You can do this, Bill. And if anybody needs to, you do."

"But I haven't been doing so good, Sam."

"You'll be fine, and we'll be back before dark. Count on it."

"What is it, Sam?" McCowen asked. "What's going on?"

"It's just the four of us, Bill. Four of us left. And if not now, when?"

After McCowen, Lombardo made three more calls. One to McCraney, one to Edith, and one to Luke Matthews, the son of a WWII buddy.

After the calls, Lombardo poured himself a jigger of grappa and slumped back on the sofa. He sipped the grappa, the pomace brandy coating his tongue and the recesses of his mouth. It burned like always, and after swallowing he winced. He didn't like grappa. But he was Italian, and Italians drank grappa. It was what they did to seal an important occasion, good or bad, a wedding or a funeral.

Lombardo downed the rest of the grappa and threw his cordial at the fake fireplace, shards of glass skittering across the parquet floor.

CHAPTER FIVE

At 4:00 AM, the alarm on Lombardo's nightstand went off. He reached blindly for the nightstand and killed it, then rolled onto his side, swinging his legs over the edge of the bed. He sat up slowly and straightened his spine. He remained motionless for a few seconds as if to nerve himself, then rocked back and forth and side to side.

Sensing equilibrium, he rocked to his feet and extended his hands to the wall for balance. He leaned forward to stretch his ankles, then bent backward and forward to stretch his lower back. A few torso twists to the right and left, followed by ten toe-rises, and as many quarter knee-bends, some of the moves producing popping sounds his chiropractor swore were released air bubbles. *Did that even make sense?*

Concluding his routine, he showered under a stream of warm water, shaved with an electric razor, and gargled with mint mouthwash. He dressed in khaki pants, his white Crispy Warriors shirt, low-cut white socks, black Rockports, and donned his WWII ballcap. Pocketing his wallet, he turned off his cellphone, placed it in a box of Kleenex, and stuffed the box in the bottom drawer of the nightstand.

In the hall at 4:45 AM, he pulled the door shut, flinching when the latch closed with the sound of a rifle cock. He squinted down both ends of the hall and smiled malevolently at two security cameras.

Tiptoeing into the atrium, dark except for a lamp on the reception desk, he focused on a figure seated at the desk—the new co-ed from Northwest Florida State College working the twelve-to-six shift, her legs propped on the desk.

Lombardo approached the sleeping co-ed, an open book on her lap and a large plastic drink cup and bag of Cheetos on the desk. He slipped the shuttle keys off the wall hook.

Outside at 4:49 AM, a chorus of frogs greeted Lombardo from the dark. A breeze of coolish air caressed his face.

He breathed deep the fragrance of morning and walked around the shuttle, parked as it always was overnight under the entrance canopy. Unlocking the door, he reached for the assist bar and climbed the three stairs, one stair at a time.

In the driver's seat, he studied the dashboard, inserted the key, closed his eyes, and turned the key. The engine came to life and idled at a low growl.

He lowered the passenger window and glanced at the main entrance. Satisfied, he released the parking brake and eased the shuttle down the narrow lane that flanked the side of the home, struck by a thought—*would anyone be there?*

Turning the corner, three shadowy figures huddled under a streetlamp halfway down the back of the home looked his direction.

He turned sharper than intended, the front wheels of the shuttle lurching, the underbelly of the shuttle scraping a concrete curb that rimmed a three-foot-wide parking lot projection. After taking out a low boxwood hedge, the shuttle settled back onto the pavement.

Pulling up to the others, all wearing old leather flight jackets, he opened the door, wearing a pasty smile. "Morning, guys."

"Great driving, slick," Beard muttered.

"Any cellphones?" Lombardo asked.

They all shook their heads.

"Perfect. Pile in."

Beard sat behind Lombardo and stowed his small grip under the seat.

Gossen assisted McCowen up the stairs and to the seat across the aisle from Beard and stowed their grips and McCowen's cane under the seat. McCowen squirmed over to the window, and Gossen sat next to him.

Lombardo glanced at his watch as he eased the shuttle from the parking lot onto Mar Walt Drive. "Five o'clock, guys. Good work. Fasten those seatbelts."

"Why are you driving, Sam?" McCowen asked. "You don't drive."

"No worries, mate. It's like riding a bike ... and it's coming back."

Beard leaned back against his neck cushion. "Yeah, obviously. Only this ain't no bike, Sam."

Gossen leaned forward, his face animated. "So, where are we headed, Sam?"

"I told you, Joe. It's a surprise. Just enjoy the ride. You'll know soon enough."

At Hurlburt Road, Lombardo turned left and then right on Eglin Parkway, the tires of the shuttle scraping the curb on each turn.

"Easy, cowboy," Beard muttered, his eyes closed. "This ain't no car, either. You got to allow for width and length. You gotta make wider turns, Sam."

******

Ten minutes later, Lombardo pulled into the Fort Walton Beach Landing Park on Santa Rosa Sound. He parked next to the only other vehicle in the lot, an olive-drab Chevy Blazer. A man got out, and Lombardo opened the shuttle door.

Beard, McCowen, and Gossen watched McCraney board the shuttle, attired in a Crispy Warrior shirt and khaki pants.

McCraney glanced from them to Lombardo. "What gives, Sam? And why the shuttle?"

Lombardo was on his feet. "I'll explain later," He pointed to the driver's seat. "But for now, TM, you're driving this tank. If you can drive an 18-wheeler, you can drive this thing."

McCraney glanced at the others, who said nothing, and slipped into the driver's seat. He scanned the dash.

"Well now, isn't this sweet. This puppy's got all the bells and whistles ... and not even 3000 miles. How'd you get it, Sam?"

"It's the home's, TM," Lombardo said, seated behind Beard. "Did you bring what I asked?"

TM retrieved a cell phone and charger from his pocket.

"Great. Keep your phone plugged in. There's a USB port up there somewhere. Keep it fully charged."

McCraney plugged the charger into the port and phone.

"Now, get us back on Highway 98 headed west toward Navarre. From there we'll take Highway 87 north to I-10."

"Where am I going?"

"West on I-10. We're going west, young man."

"I mean, where are we going?"

"I'll let you know when we get there."

McCraney glanced at the others. Gossen shrugged ignorance. Beard and McCowen were asleep.

On Highway 98, traffic was light, and soon Gossen was asleep.

McCraney eyed Lombardo in the rearview window. "So, tell me, Sam. How did you get the shuttle?"

"I borrowed it, TM."

"You borrowed it? You don't just borrow a shuttle."

Lombardo didn't respond.

"Is this on the up and up, Sam? What's this all about?"

Lombardo still didn't answer.

Stopping for a red light at Doolittle Boulevard, McCraney craned his neck around. "Listen, Sam, I don't know what you're up to, and I'm not sure I want to. You said meet you at the landing, and I did, and I didn't question the Crispy Warrior shirt. You told me you were going to show me Charlie's favorite fishing hole. Got my rods, tackle, and everything in the Blazer. You never said anything about the guys or us going somewhere."

"Relax, TM. We'll fish Charlie's hole. Just not today."

"You stole it. Didn't you, Sam? The shuttle."

"Stole it? Of course not. It's part of what we pay for at the home. We just didn't need a driver."

"You're joking, right?"

Beard stirred.

"Look, Sam, you might see this as a joke—a hoot for you dinosaurs. But I don't. I still have to make a living. No telling where this is going. Except it won't be good. I don't want any part of it."

"You're overreacting, TM. It's going to be fine. You'll see."

"The inside of a jail, maybe."

"Not going to happen. When they finally figure out it's us with the shuttle, they're not going to know anything about you. How could they? You're squeaky clean. And I'm going to keep you that way."

"And just how are you going to do that?"

CHAPTER SIX

Heading west on Hwy 98, the shuttle skirted Hurlburt Field at 5:30 AM, the first light of dawn quenching the darkness. Lombardo's eyes were outside the shuttle. He hadn't seen a single police, sheriff, or highway patrol car. Quiescent strip malls, convenience stores, gas stations, auto repair shops, churches, schools, billboards, and acres of scrub oaks and palmettos flanked both sides of the road.

At 5:50 AM the shuttle entered the sleepy village of Navarre, Florida, and Lombardo was on his feet, the others asleep, mouths open, snoring lightly.

At the front of the shuttle, he winked at McCraney and loosed a shrill whistle that animated the shuttle.

"What the hell?" Beard growled.

Despite not wanting to McCraney grinned.

"Check it out boys! The golden hour! Got us one beautiful day. Just for us. Not a cloud in the sky."

McCowen rubbed his eyes. "I need some grub, Sam."

Beard stretched his arms. "I could do a coffee."

"I'll take both," Gossen said. "But not until I pee."

"Should be something here in Navarre, TM. Do a Mickey D's or whatever comes up. I'm buying!"

"The least you can do," McCraney muttered.

Pulling out of McDonald's at 6:05 AM with bladders empty and food bags and drinks, Beard a coffee, McCraney drove north on Highway 87, slowing to a crawl through stretches of dense ground fog. Thirty-five minutes later, he goosed the shuttle up the ramp to I-10 West.

27

As Lombardo swallowed the last of a second sausage egg biscuit, he grimaced at an 18-wheeler overtaking the shuttle. "What's with the sixty-five, TM? Gotta be seventy-five or we'll never get there."

McCraney goosed the gas.

"Give us a hint, Sam," McCowen said. "At least let us guess, then you tell us if we're right."

"No can do, Bill," Lombardo said. "Not going to spoil it."

A wry smile crossed Beard's face. "Not necessary, boys. I know exactly where we're going."

Lombardo ignored Beard.

"Yep, got it figured out, Sam. I know where we're going, and I'll lay a fiver on it."

"I'll take that bet," Gossen said. "So, where are we going?"

"Nope, not yet, Joe. I'll tell you when we exit."

Minutes later, after crossing Blackwater Bay, all eyes outside the window, Lombardo saw the exit sign for Milton and Bagdad, wondering what he always wondered when he saw the sign. *How in the world does a town in northwest Florida get the name Bagdad?*

When the shuttle reached the long bridge over Escambia Bay the sun was high enough to cast a million silvery shimmers across the rippling bay.

Beyond the bridge, the shuttle skirted north Pensacola and passed the exit for the Naval Air Museum.

"Sam, state line coming up," McCraney piped nervously. "You didn't say anything about leaving the state."

"It's all good, TM. Just drive normal."

"No, Sam. It is not all good. Crossing the state line—that brings in the Feds. The FBI, Sam. Talking, interstate trafficking … or whatever they call it. Federal prison. I'm not doing that for you or anybody."

McCraney suddenly stood on the brakes. "Sam! State trooper coming up fast!"

Lombardo whirled about. McCrancy was right.

A Florida state trooper approached at high speed. Looming large in the left lane as if to pass, the trooper abruptly pulled into the right lane behind the shuttle.

"Where is he, Sam? I don't see him."

"He's behind us, TM. Just be cool. He's not flashing his lights. Were you speeding?"

"Doing what you told me. On seventy now."

"Then no problem, right? Just stay cool and keep your eye on the road."

Two miles from the Alabama state line, the trooper shifted to the left lane and pulled alongside the shuttle.

"Sheesh, Sam," No way this gonna end up right!" McCraney squealed.

Lombardo eyed the officer riding shotgun; black, burly, and sporting aviator shades.

"What's he doing, Sam?"

"Checking us out, TM. The Minute Man gets everyone."

Lombardo saw Beard waving at the officer. He pressed his chest against the window and pointed to his shirt.

After a few seconds, the trooper nodded back.

Approaching the Perdido River bridge, Beard rendered the trooper a sharp salute.

"Sorry, TM," Lombardo said. "No turning back now."

The trooper applied his brakes, crossed the median just short of the bridge, and headed east on I-10.

"Hallelujah, sweet Jesus," McCraney shouted. "Hallelujah, amen! Father, forgive me my sins but not my brainless brother's."

As they crossed the bridge, Lombardo barked, "Back on seventy-five, TM. Eighty, if a rabbit comes along."

Gossen glimpsed wistfully at the Alabama Welcome Center. "I gotta pee, Sam."

"Joe, you're killing me. TM, pull over. Five-minutes! No more. Anyone not on the bus gets picked up on the way back. We're on a mission, men. Maybe our last. And we're going to finish it."

******

En route to Spanish Fort after the pit stop, McCraney's cell phone rang.

"That'll be for me, TM," Lombardo said, on his feet. He raised the phone to his ear, his finger to his lips.

"This is Sam … Hey, girl. Oh, yeah, that's right. That's just how we say it, *Commo check*. Gotta make sure we can hear each other. And I got you loud and clear. Keep your eyes open and let me know as soon as something happens. Okay? Thanks."

Lombardo handed McCraney the phone. "That, boys, was Edith. She's our eyes and ears on the inside. And everything's quiet. All good."

*****

Five minutes later McCraney's phone rang again, and Lombardo was on his feet.

"Uh huh. Really?" Lombardo grinned as Edith talked. "When? They haven't? I'll bet she is. Talk her down if you can. But don't tell her anything."

Lombardo winked at the others.

"Gotcha, girl. That makes sense. I will. Great work, Edith. Thanks. And to think, all this time I thought you were just another dazzling dame."

A Cheshire grin crossed Lombardo's face as he hung up.

"Veronica is all kinds of pissed, and Scotty's hot as hell. But nobody suspects us."

"Yeah, like who would?" Beard said. "So, that's it?"

"Not quite. The police and sheriff know the shuttle's missing and are on the lookout."

"I told you, Sam," McCraney's tone turned tenor. "I am so screwed. Driving a stolen vehicle, kidnapping four halfwits, and crossing state lines."

Lombardo turned to Gossen. "Johanna is a bit ruffled, Joe. When you weren't in the dining room for breakfast, she told Veronica. They both think you wandered off campus." Lombardo smothered a grin. "You do that a lot?"

CHAPTER SEVEN

"Sam," McCowen said, "this makes no sense. TM's right. We don't stand a chance. Once the word gets out—a shuttle with a Minute Man plastered on the side—we'll be easy pickings. Turn around now, and they'll chalk it up to senility."

Lombardo glared at McCowen as if he had suggested castration.

"You are kidding. Right?"

McCowen didn't respond.

"Turn around? You want to just turn around? Tail between our legs. Snivel back to the holding pen?"

Beard and Gossen exchanged glances as Lombardo's words hung in the air.

"Sam," Gossen ventured timorously, "Bill's just saying, if we don't stand a chance, why—"

"No, Joe! Not only no, but hell no. We're not going back until we have our day in the sun. Is that too much to ask?"

Silence.

"Think of it." Lombardo's eyes flashed. "We go back now, what happens?"

Silence.

"I'll tell you what happens. We're the laughingstock of the home. Like TM said, just four old fossils that got a hair up their ass and wandered off the reservation. Now that really is senility."

McCowen shifted in his seat. "Well, at least tell us where we're going, Sam?"

Beard stood up. "Going to Biloxi, guys. That's where we're going." He winked at Lombardo. "Got to be Biloxi. Sam loves blackjack, maybe more than me. We've been twice on the tour bus that comes to the home. My guess, Beaux Rivage like last time. Right, Sam? Huge and beautiful. With all the glitz of Vegas."

Lombardo stood stone-faced, tight-lipped.

"Besides, Sam's right. Like it or not, we can't undo what we've done. That he conned us into this, is on us. I say we ride it out, see what happens."

"Exactly," Lombardo said. "Turn around now, and our one chance is gone. Nothing changes. Everything's the same. The four of us skulking around the home, stalking the halls, caged in our rooms, watching TVs that suck the brain cells right out our eyeballs, and—God save us—lining up for bingo."

Beard shot Lombardo a look. "Now wait a minute, Sam. Nothing wrong with bingo. It's America's game. Like Wheel of Fortune."

******

After ten minutes of dead silence, all eyes outside the shuttle, McCraney's phone rang again, Lombardo on his feet.

"Hey, Edith. Uh-huh. She did?" Lombardo glanced at Gossen. "Tell her I just called and Joe's with me, Bill, and John. One of the Crispies picked us up for a day trip, and we'll be back for supper. Sure, tell Veronica too. Anything else? Oh? Really? This is great intel, Edith. You are doing a super job. You're wearing your hearing aids? Good. Stay close to Veronica. We need to know as soon as she suspects us. Got to run, girl."

Lombardo handed the phone to McCraney.

"All good?" Beard asked.

"Well, they still don't suspect us."

McCraney prayed in a whisper. "Lord, protect us from ourselves."

Lombardo turned to Gossen. "You heard what I said? About Edith talking Johanna down?"

Gossen nodded.

"And that's it?" Beard said.

"Not exactly. The State Troopers know. We dodged a bullet."

As the shuttle sped west through the pinewood landscape between the Alabama border and Mobile Bay, Lombardo counted billboards for the same personal injury attorneys. He was up to four.

Suddenly on his feet, he shuffled to the front, squeezed McCraney's shoulders, and spun round, his eyes dancing in their sockets. "Can you believe it, boys? We are actually doing this!"

The grin on his face morphed to a chuckle, the chuckle to a chortle, the chortle to a horselaugh that infected Beard, McCowen, and Gossen, guffaws filling the shuttle, except from the driver's seat.

Catching his breath, Lombardo slapped McCraney on the back. "I know, TM, this is some kind of stupid. We're idiots. But we're alive! Alive like I can't remember."

"TM," Gossen said. "Don't worry. No way Sam won't keep you clean."

Lombardo's eyes shined. "Boys, we are going to see this through."

With that, Beard raised a hand. "Been thinking about what you said, Sam."

"How's that?"

"About this being a mission. The four of us on a mission."

"So now I don't even count?" McCraney muttered.

"Of course, you count, TM. But this sort of reminds me of my first mission."

"Flying a B-25?" McCowen asked.

"No. That would come later. More than ten years later. No, I'm talking about before the war. Before I joined the Army."

Gossen expressed confusion. "You'd have been a kid."

"None of you know about my growing up years," Beard said. "Just like I don't know about yours, except for Sam coming over on the boat."

The older of the two centenarians ambled to the front of the shuttle, Lombardo taking his seat.

Beard rubbed his hands together, his eyes twinkling. "We've all got stories, right? And mine's no more special than yours. Just different. Old Sam here has his Ellis Island story. Escaping Italy and fascism to come to where he still can't speak the language."

Gossen chuckled.

"But you've made an amazing life of it, Sam. You really are one of a kind. Your impact on people, your life, your story—amazing."

Lombardo waved him off.

"But we've got a ways to go before Biloxi, so if you want, maybe I can eat up some time."

Beard's impish grin made an appearance.

"What if I told you, you're looking at the youngest hobo ever to ride the rails?"

CHAPTER EIGHT

Beard described his early life, beginning with his birth in December of 1918, a month after what was to be called the Great War. His father had scratched out a living on a small farm in western West Virginia, the poorest part of a poor state. His mother died when he was two, his father when he was six. His father being a member of the Odd Fellows, his uncle took him to the Odd Fellows orphanage near Elkins, West Virginia.

Lombardo, skeptical, crossed his arms. "You're pulling my legs, John."

"Leg, Sam. Not legs. And whether you believe it or not, it's the God's honest truth. I couldn't make this up."

"Uncanny," Gossen said. "That you were orphaned, John. I wasn't orphaned, but I never knew my biological mother."

"So, what happened, John," McCowen pressed.

"The orphanage was huge, beautiful." Beard spread his arms wide. "Seemed to me a palace and located on more than a hundred acres just outside of town. Had maybe a hundred kids. I have an old photograph of it in my apartment I'll show you. Lots of rooms, wood paneling, high ceilings, chandeliers, and it covered the entire top of a hill. Open spaces and woods all around. Big trees. Great climbing trees. Us boys had two dorm rooms, rows of bunks with lockers. The girls also had two. They kept us separate for school and otherwise."

"What was it like," Gossen asked, "being in an orphanage?"

"Okay, I guess. Overnight, I had new brothers and sisters. The food was alright, and there was always enough of it. Which was saying something in those days. The Depression and all. I finished grade school there, and all the time, especially the last two years, hung out

"

with the older boys. We'd fish the nearby river—more like a stream, except when it flooded—and played a lot of baseball. Only had one bat and a couple of old raggedy balls. Nobody had a glove."

McCowen grinned. "Serious sand lot."

"It was. And it was my home and stayed my home until I opened my big fat mouth the summer after sixth grade. That would have been," Beard thought for a moment, "1931, I think. Tough times everywhere, but not so bad at the orphanage."

"The worst of times," McCowen murmured to himself.

"I was keen on this one girl," Beard said. "She was about my age, cute as a button, and I don't know why, but she liked me. We traded notes, and when no one was looking, we held hands. Don't know that we ever kissed.

"One day I was with these older boys, and one of them says nobody has ever run away from the orphanage, like no one ever would."

Lombardo still wasn't buying it.

"Don't ask me why, but I up and say, *I'll do it. I'll be the first.* Why I said it, I'll never know. Except maybe to impress the girl. The big kids just ignored me. But, me, I thought about it for days. And kept thinking about it. I told the girl what I'd said, and she said, *Don't you dare do it, John Beard. That's the stupidest thing I ever heard.* And of course she was right."

"You were how old?" Lombardo asked, a chink in his disbelief.

"Twelve. And all full of myself, the smartest kid in my class. The railroad ran close to the orphanage on its way into Elkins. There was a hobo camp not a mile from the orphanage, near a sharp bend in the river where the trains had to slow to a crawl. That's where the hobos would jump, either on or off. Always a tricky business. I had watched them do it. Me and some friends fished that stretch a lot and nerved ourselves to visit the camp a couple of times. One time, we snuck them food from the dining hall."

Gossen's jaw dropped. "You really did it? You hopped a train?"

"Only meant to be gone overnight. Just long enough to be missed. Then come back the next day the conquering hero, take my licks and get the girl."

Lombardo grinned ear to ear.

"It wasn't funny, Sam. The first thing you learn about being a hobo is you got a lot to learn about being a hobo. Like, you never ride a train all the way into a station. That's where the agents are—the railroad agents. And these guys aren't paid to be nice. Anyway, I hopped a train. Ate what I'd brought in the first hour and fell asleep in a box car. Something about the rhythm of a train. Rode it all the way into the Baltimore switchyard and woke up the next morning hungry."

McCraney glanced at Beard through the rearview mirror. "You were one dumbass kid, John."

"Yeah, I was. Slid the car door open, jumped out, and wasn't on the ground ten seconds before this big guy with a Billy club rounds the car. I start running in the opposite direction, right into another agent."

Lombardo stared in amazement. "You really did this?"

"I swear it's true, Sam. Not even a teenager, and I'm in a jail cell for three weeks, with the drunks hauled in each night to sleep it off. We got one meal a day. Seriously, one meal. A sandwich with some sort of meat—always full of fat and gristle and stuffed between two hard-as-rock slices of brown moldy bread. And the water they gave us smelled of bad eggs and tasted worse."

McCraney winced.

"Finally, after a couple of weeks of them wondering what to do with me, and me clamoring about being an orphan and taking a dare, one of the deputies called the orphanage."

"Thank God," Gossen said with relief.

"I had hoped so," Beard said. "The director, he liked me well enough, and he was a fair man. But he was strict. Had to be. I never got to talk to him ... not directly. The deputy did all the talking, asked all the questions. After he hung up, he told me the orphanage couldn't take me back, that the director wished me luck."

McCowen stared at Beard, unblinking. "You're kidding."

"No. The deputy told me the director had no choice, that since I was a runaway and had a jail record, it was out of his hands."

"Deep kimchi," McCraney muttered.

"Yep. And believe what you want, after I promised not to do it again, they set me free, and I rode the trains for eight, almost nine years, until I joined the Army Air Corps in 1940. As much a hobo as any hobo. And me just a kid. At first anyway."

"This would make a great movie," Gossen said.

"Don't know about that, but for sure I got me a different kind of education. And it's served me well." Beard winked at Lombardo. "Every day was like being on a mission. Always looking for work, for food to eat, clothes to wear, a place to sleep, especially in the winter ... hard times."

"How is it we never heard any of this?" McCowen asked.

Beard shrugged. "Nobody asked."

"That must have screwed with your mind," Gossen said. "You running the rails with a bunch of shady characters."

"Shady? Maybe some, but very few. People today wouldn't understand. A hobo, at that time anyway, wasn't a bum standing on a street corner holding a sign or waiting for a handout. Far from it. Most had families. There just wasn't any work, or enough work. You had to go looking for it. You rode trains, hitchhiked, or walked from town to town. And hobos, the ones I rode with, had a code of ethics. Anyone who didn't follow the rules or do his part didn't share in what was found to eat or otherwise. I knew of some that got kicked out of camp.

"The older guys liked me and looked out for me, mostly because I was useful. I had a way of getting folks to share what they had—and back then nobody had much. I never asked for anything without offering to work for it. None of us did. We did whatever needed doing. Painting, chopping wood, mending fence, fixing what was broke, working the fields, gardens ... anything."

"Almost sounds like fun," Gossen mused. "Doing something different every day."

"It wasn't, Joe. I remember days with nothing to eat. And not a day went by I didn't want to go back to the orphanage. Seemed I was always hungry or cold or both."

"Unbelievable," McCraney said. "Even if only some of it is true. How many hobos were there?"

"My daughter, Kerry, did an internet search. Said there were four million. I was always in a group of not more than twenty. Every city or town with a railroad running through it had at least one hobo camp. And somewhere in the camp, hanging from a tree, would be a black iron cauldron or some sort of pot for cooking an evening meal—whatever was scrounged."

"The hobo stew?" McCraney suggested.

"Not what you think, TM. But food was food. I don't know that we ever expected more than one decent meal a day. Though, like I say, too often, not even one. Don't know that I ever saw a fat hobo."

"Eight years," McCowen mused. "How many trains did you ride?"

"I've given it a lot of thought, Bill. But I never kept track. Had to be hundreds. Maybe a thousand. Seemed like I was always on the move." Beard's impish grin made an appearance. "But I was never nabbed a second time by a railroad agent. Traveled as far south as the Florida Keys, as far west as Texas, and always back north to West Virginia and Pennsylvania. And did it over and over again, spending the winters in the south."

Abandoning his skepticism, Lombardo asked, "You ever go back to the orphanage?"

"Thought about it all the time. Even got close a few times. But, no, I never did. Been eighty-seven years now since I last saw the place. It might not even be there now."

"John Beard," McCraney declared, "the good Lord has been looking out for you."

"You think? Or maybe I've just been lucky. I've never been much into religion. Anyway, that's my story. It's time we heard from someone else."

"Not so fast, John," McCowen insisted. "You can't leave us there. How did you go from being a hobo with a grade school education to flying bombers for the Army Air Corps and retiring a Lieutenant Colonel?"

CHAPTER NINE

"All right then," Beard said, obliging McCowen. "The short of it, when the war heated up, I heard you got three hot meals a day in the military. So, I went to a recruiter and said I wanted to serve my country, and did he have a job for me. You have to remember, by this time I'm pretty good at reading people and situations and how to tackle a thing. I chat him up, and he asked if I knew anything about machines and engines and how they worked. I said I did because I'd become quite the mechanic as a hobo. Loved tinkering with motors and such.

"He suggested the Army Air Corps, that they needed mechanics. I said that would be fine with me. Then he asked if I had a high school diploma. Early on they required it, and that should have been the end of it. But I looked him straight in the eye and said, *doesn't everyone?* Apparently, he checked the box that I did, and the rest is history. He enlisted me in the Army Air Corps. Said I would be going to aircraft maintenance school to become a crew chief."

Lombardo's grin turned to laughter. "Knowing you the way I do, John, how could I not believe this?"

"But flying and becoming an officer?" Gossen pressed.

"A sixth-grade education was something back then, at least at the orphanage. The rest was just street smarts."

"That doesn't answer my question. You were enlisted, right?"

"Yep. When I finished maintenance school, I was a private making $30 a month, more money than I'd ever seen, and fattening up on all those meals. But not long after, the Air Corps finds itself short on pilots, they put out a call for enlisted men with aptitude to become sergeant pilots."

"Never heard of a sergeant pilot," Lombardo said.

"Not many have, and the program didn't last more than a few months. Anyway, the first sergeant picked me and bumped me to buck sergeant, the minimum rank for the program. I went to flight school and finished near the top of the class. They asked what I wanted to fly, and I said bombers. Right off, I was assigned to a B-25 bomber squadron, the Doolittle plane that bombed Tokyo.

"Before I'm even checked out in the plane, a flight of eight new B-25s was to be ferried to North Africa, to Egypt, and one of the assigned pilots pulled up sick. They asked for a volunteer, and I raised my hand. Don't recall anyone else raising a hand. Next thing I know, I'm the co-pilot on a B-25 flying to South America, then across the Atlantic with a stop in the Ascension Islands. After we arrived on the gold coast of Africa, we flew north to Egypt. Along the way, the command pilot taught me to fly the bird, and we split the flying time."

Beard paused. "Two of the planes didn't make it across the Atlantic."

"You're unbelievable, John," Lombardo said. "A grade school education and then a pilot."

"Yep. Bumped me to staff sergeant on graduation and paid me twice what I got as a crew chief."

"But how did you become a commissioned officer?" McCowen asked.

"Battlefield commission, Bill. The only sergeant pilot ever to get one. The rest, those that survived, were made warrant officers."

"How'd you get it?" Gossen asked.

"During my first combat tour in North Africa, we were flying close air support for the British and later the Americans when they arrived. Mostly targeting Rommel's Afrika Korps."

McCowen blinked in disbelief. "Wait. You flew more than one combat tour, when you could have gone home? Been out of the war?"

"Actually, two more. Remember, I had no better place to go. In my second tour, we covered the Allied invasion of Sicily and then Italy. My third tour was in the China-Burma-India theater, the CBI, fighting the Japanese. No one talks much about that piece of the war, but it was a nasty business. Nasty. You didn't want to bail out in Jap-controlled territory."

"You're certifiably nuts, John Beard," Lombardo declared.

"Did you ever get any additional schooling?" Gossen asked.

Beard produced another impish grin. "Nope. Not unless you count what I learned to be a stockbroker."

CHAPTER TEN

**WWII, China-Burma-India (CBI) Theater, June 1944
An Airfield near the Eastern Border of India**

On the groundman's signal, Captain John Beard flipped the magneto switches that powered the B-25's two 1700 HP Wright Cyclone engines, the backwash dusting the three bombers behind him.

He taxied to the takeoff apron where another B-25 was revving its engines. He waved at the pilot in the other plane who would be flying close air support for Merrill's Marauders near Myitkyina, what Beard had done two days earlier.

In the early morning climb out to the east, Beard squinted into a brilliant sunrise, despite wearing tinted flight glasses. In the right seat, First Lieutenant Frank Phillips, his co-pilot, lit up. Second Lieutenant Jim Wilson, navigator/bombardier, huddled with a nautical chart in the cramped plexiglass nose bubble below the cockpit. That was it, just a three-man crew for a plane designed for five.

Phillips and Wilson bantered over the intercom about the baseball game played two nights earlier. A fundraiser at the Polo Grounds between the New York Yankees, Brooklyn Dodgers, and New York Giants. The first ever three-team baseball game. Word was that the game raised more than five million dollars in war bonds, the Dodgers winning, scoring five runs in three innings at bat.

At 8000 feet, Beard leveled off, synched the propellers, and throttled back to a cruising speed of 230 miles per hour.

"Heading 115, boss," Wilson said. "Estimated time to target seventy-five minutes."

"Roger that," Beard said, trimming the aircraft and slowly, almost lovingly, thumbing circles around the two buttons on his control yoke.

His eyes continually searched the sky and the instrument panel. He caught Phillips staring at his thumb. One of the buttons fired six 50-caliber machine guns from the nose of the aircraft. The other dropped "eggs," 500 or 1000-pound bombs, from the bomb bay.

"So, what do you think, sir?" Phillips asked.

"Just another day of war, Phillips."

"Not what I heard in the briefing."

"Nothing we can't handle."

"No one else could."

Despite his own misgivings, Beard let it go. The target had been assigned four times and still stood untouched. But they wouldn't know more until they saw it for themselves.

A quarter hour later passed, and they were over Japanese-controlled Burma. Hawk-like, Beard scanned the surreal landscape.

He'd never seen anything like it. The size of Texas, nothing like Africa, Sicily, or Italy, it was a British possession, kite-like with a long tail trailing south. Abutting the Himalayas to the north, where forbidding snow-capped peaks approached 20,000 feet, it deflated southwards to the Andaman Sea.

Below them and on the east side of the country's Central Basin everything was either up or down. Nothing flat. Jungle coated, razor-sharp ridges, bottomless valleys. As if a giant hand had clutched the earth, wrinkling it like a paper fan.

Far below, bridges, rail and otherwise, transected tributaries to the Irrawaddy and other rivers and served up daily targets. Today's mission, like most, destroy another bridge, sever Japanese supply lines. He'd lost track of how many they'd notched in the last two months, sometimes as many as three a day. Most had been easy marks, the tactics straightforward. A high-level flyover to reconnoiter the target and its defenses, then a low-level, thirty-degree angled attack run lengthwise on the bridge, laying an egg or two on the deck, followed by whatever maneuvers necessary to elude enemy ordnance. And, so far, only scratches.

But the morning briefing suggested otherwise. The target was a short stubby bridge connecting two sharply steep ridges. Too short for a classic attack.

Phillips extinguished his cigarette against the aircraft frame. "Why are you still here, Captain? Three tours? More than a hundred combat missions. I mean, who the hell does that?"

Beard stared straight ahead. "A halfwit, I suppose. Or … someone tired of trains."

"Trains, sir?"

"You've got something going on, don't you Phillips?" Beard said."

"Sir?"

"Every time I pass your bunk, the perfume from your locker knocks me over."

"Letters, sir … from my sister."

Beard gave him a look.

Phillips laughed. "Okay, okay. It's that nurse in Italy—you remember the one?"

"I do."

"We've still got it on. She wants to see New York if I make it."

"You have doubts?'

"Not as many as I did, sir. A lot of the guys say you're the best in the group. I mean, you haven't lost a plane or a man, and Jim and I are starting to think we might actually make it."

"That's a fact, boss," Wilson chimed over the intercom. "And if there is anything, I mean anything, we can do to make your life easier, you just let us know."

Beard grinned as he re-synced the propellers.

"And if we do survive," Phillips added, "you won't find me or Wilson hanging around."

"Especially me, boss," Wilson chimed. "Not after I was cheated. All I got was two weeks in Italy. The weather perfect, the wine amazing—and all those chicks. And then they send us to the CBI, where it's either British gin or tea, or worse than that, Indian gin or tea, and the weather's either too damn hot and dry, or too damn hot and wet. Hell, I'm already soaked. And I got this bug I can't shake. I can't pass up a crapper."

Beard wiped his forehead with an already soaked handkerchief. "What's our position, Wilson?"

"Getting close, sir. We cross the Irrawaddy in twenty. Should have the target in another ten."

A puff of white smoke appeared off the left wing, spawning a well-oiled obscenity from Wilson.

Another puff—closer—with the attendant orange flash and black finish.

"There, sir," Phillips said. "Down there. One o'clock. Top of the ridge."

Another airburst shook the fuselage. Beard banked hard to the left and then cut a series of S-turns until well past the ridge. Strange, he thought, despite the Allies turning the tide of the war and owning the skies, the Japanese still owned most of the ground.

"Your plane, Phillips," Beard said.

Phillips took the yoke, and Beard studied the aerial photograph and topographic map passed out at the morning briefing, a red X marking the target on each. The aerial photograph was useless, taken too high, there was no evidence of a bridge or anything but jungle around the red X.

He focused on the topographic map. It showed a bridge beneath the red X and a rail line crossing between steep ridges, the ridges a thousand feet high.

"I don't like it, sir," Phillips muttered. "If we attack straight on, they'll hear us coming a mile out."

"Yep," Beard muttered as he studied the contours on the topographic map, eyeing what struck him as an anomaly on the ridge west of the bridge.

"My plane," he said, handing Phillips the topographic map.

"The ridge west of the bridge, maybe a quarter mile short of the bridge. What do you see?"

Phillips studied the map. "A steep-ass ridge, sir ... with what looks like … I'm not sure … a saddle?"

"That's my read. Assuming the map's right, we'll come in low up the adjacent valley. Behind a wall of granite, they shouldn't hear us. You got that, Wilson?"

"Gotcha, boss." Wilson had one eye on an aeronautical chart, the other on what lay ahead of them.

Beard observed the Irrawaddy River passing beneath them. Massive, it was Southeast Asia's Mississippi, and despite the war, teeming with junks.

Beyond the river, Wilson announced, "Two minutes, boss." A minute and a half later. "Next ridge, boss."

Beard drew in a deep breath, *show time.*

He banked the aircraft hard left, the G-forces pinning the crew against their seats. He slipped the bird in a steep descent, nearly shaving the ridge wall before leveling out just above tree-top and flying nap-of-the-earth through airspace no more than fifty-yards wide.

The right wingtip clipped a tree branch.

"Shitake, boss!" Wilson squawked.

Seconds later, the valley widened.

"There, sir." Phillips pointed. "Up there."

Beard already spied it, the saddle high and on the right. He shoved the throttles full forward and pulled hard on the yoke. "Remind me to buy our mapmaker whatever he's drinking. Wilson, open the bomb bay."

As the gears of the bomb bay screeched, Beard executed a sharp right turn through the saddle, just feet above a field of jagged boulders. On the other side of the ridge, he banked hard left.

"There, sir!" Phillips pointed. "That's our bridge."

Directly in front of them and five hundred feet below, a short, trestled bridge connected the steep valley walls, parapeted defenses at either end, trucks and personnel crossing the bridge. He plunged the nose of the aircraft in a swerving dive, firing short machinegun bursts at the parapets and figures scurrying for cover.

In the seconds before reaching the bridge, machinegun fire pinged the bomber, two rounds piercing the plexiglass nose of the plane.

"Son of a bitch!" Wilson shouted.

Fifty feet from the bridge, Beard pressed the other button and initiated a steep climb.

With almost no hangtime, the 1000-lb egg landed squarely on the bridge deck, the fireball sending fragments of bridge and everything else in all directions, tickling the bird's tail feathers.

"Bullseye, boss!" Wilson hollered. "Nothing but bullseye. You did it, sir. You're amazing!"

At altitude, Beard leveled off and banked the aircraft for a damage assessment. Where the bridge had been, a stream flowed, dotted with white rapids.

"God Bless you, sir." Phillips giggled nervously. "We're still alive."

"Then, why don't you take us home, Phillips."

CHAPTER ELEVEN

"You're right, John," McCowen said. "We each have a story. And by all rights none of us should be here, save for the grace of God … or," He wagged a finger at Beard. "Fate."

"You mean like you being pitched through the nose of that B-29 with barely a scratch," Lombardo said, recalling the story McCowen's son, Clint, had told at a Crispy Warrior breakfast after he circulated photographs of the crash wreckage. The photos defied any survivors, yet all but one of the crew survived.

At the breakfast, McCowen kept silent, his son doing all the talking. He spoke of his father flying for the Strategic Air Command, known as SAC, first flying the B-29 in the Korean War, then the B-47, and finally the B-52 Stratofortress, including eight years of twenty-four-hour missions carrying six thermonuclear bombs with Moscow as his target.

He also spoke of the time the entire east coast was shut down for a landing gear failure when his father was returning from a Moscow mission. Flying on fumes in a thunderstorm after being diverted to a foamed runway, he had landed in a severe crosswind, the wingtip of the massive bird scraping the ground.

"What did you fly in WWII, Bill?" McCraney asked.

"Wasn't a pilot then, TM. I really wanted to be, but just seventeen, I wanted in like everyone else and enlisted and became a gunner. I didn't get to Italy until near the end of the war. While I waited for a squadron assignment, I watched the Germans bomb Naples night after night."

"How old were you?"

"By then, eighteen."

"Then we're about the same age," Gossen said. "I know you flew SAC missions and after retiring out of Hurlburt stayed in the Fort Walton Beach area, but where were you born?"

"New York. Most of my growing up years in Cornwall-on-Hudson. Just north of West Point, the Military Academy."

"Sounds idyllic," Beard said.

McCowen smiled cynically. "Hearing your story, mine's got a similar ring. About the Depression, anyway."

"Then let's hear it," Lombardo declared. "You're on." "Okay."

McCowen smiled at Beard. "To begin with, I never hopped a train. Though the thought of getting away from home was always on my mind. I was one of seven siblings, five brothers and a sister. Mother raised us, a saint of a woman, as we were pretty much abandoned by my father, a mechanic. During the Depression he was off looking for work—like John said, everybody looking for work. And to his credit, he sent money home when he could. But we never had much. In fact, I think we were the poorest family in Cornwall."

McCowen glanced at his feet.

"Any of you ever have to put cardboard in your shoes to go to school or play?"

"I did," McCraney said.

"Then, you know what I'm talking about. And don't get me wrong. New York was and is an amazing, beautiful state, but it's not like Florida. The seasons are real. Half the year it's cold to frigid, lots of snow. The Hudson River freezes over for months. But the McCowens always managed through the Depression, the church helping us with shoes, clothes, and such. I was always big, or at least tall, for my age, over six feet by the time I was thirteen, and good at sports—soccer, basketball, and baseball. I had to be. That's how I got decent shoes."

"Shoes?" Gossen repeated.

"I lettered fourteen times playing for Cornwall High School and was on the all-star basketball and soccer teams. A big deal for my self-esteem. But an even bigger deal for my feet. I don't recall ever having new clothes or shoes, except for my basketball shoes, which I wore to class … every day. Everything else was hand-me-downs or charity."

"I would never have guessed, Bill," Lombardo said.

"No complaints, Sam. God has obviously blessed me in so many ways, then and since. Anyway, after WWII, I got out and did the G.I. Bill thing at the University of Denver. I loved to draw and paint and intended to be an architect. But then, I got back in the service to fly planes. While in school, I met Beverly Fryer— the love of my life— beautiful and former Miss Nevada. She was a high-level executive secretary for the government, smarter than me. We married in '47 and had three boys. You, of course, know Clint from Crispy Warriors. I continued to fly and retired in 1969 at Eglin and started a construction company and started building homes. After 64 wonderful years, I lost Beverly in 2011. You would have loved her."

"I'm sure we would have," Gossen said. "How many homes did you build?"

"A lot. Over five hundred. And I started a chain of oil and lube service centers in 1982. But most recently I've been working with son Clint on his idea to harvest energy from the atmosphere."

"Energy?" Gossen asked, puzzled.

"It's complicated, Joe. If you want, I'll have him send you some information. It's really his deal."

"I heard Clint talking about it," Lombardo said. "Something about extracting energy from thin air."

"That's right. He fills me in on his thinking, and I give him feedback."

"You think it's possible?" Lombardo asked.

McCowen grinned. "If he does, I do."

Lombardo winked. "Maybe you can slip me a few shares when you go public."

"In your military career," Beard said, "would you say flying for SAC was the highlight?"

McCowen was slow to answer. "No. Not necessarily. After fifteen years flying for SAC and all the hemorrhoids, the Air Force put out an urgent request for experienced pilots to fly in Vietnam. I volunteered and flew the C-123."

"The C-123?" That's quite a step down. A small piston-plane, right?"

"That's the one, John. A high wing twin-engine plane with amazing short field takeoff and landing capabilities. Handled like a small Cessna. I carried troops, supplies, dropped flares, whatever was needed. It was blast to fly, and we never really knew what to expect when we landed or took off. It could get into a lot of tight places and take a lot of punishment."

CHAPTER TWELVE

South Vietnam—Ia Drang Valley— November 14-15, 1965

Captain Randall Blake, Operations Officer for the 310th Air Commando Squadron, entered the Quonset hut briefing room at Camp Holloway outside of Pleiku in the Central Highlands of II Corps. His brow knit, he eyed Major Bill McCowen sitting on the front row.

McCowen focused on the large black briefing board chalked up with the day's operations and intelligence information. Seated beside him was Captain Stan Ward, his co-pilot and the only other man in the briefing room. McCowen's attention shifted to the large acetate-covered aerial photograph of the Central Highlands, a composite of a dozen smaller photographs.

Blake opened his folder and sorted through notes while McCowen and Ward scribbled information on their kneepad clipboards —weather conditions, frequencies, intelligence.

"Gentlemen," Blake began, "if you haven't heard, it all started this morning. Our first-ever aerial insertion of a battalion-size unit by a bevy of UH-1 Hueys. Colonel Hal Moore's 1st Battalion of the 7th Cavalry inserted east of the Chu Pong massif at Landing Zone X-Ray, a clearing about the size of a football field and surrounded by rainforest, thick jungle, and tall elephant grass, and, of course, the Chu Pong massif on one side."

Blake turned to the acetate-covered map and tapped the location of LZ X-Ray, circled in red.

"As you can see, Moore's forces sit at the foot of Chu Pong Mountain. Its peak is 2400 feet and not five miles from the Cambodian border. Intelligence reports that two North Vietnamese Army regiments are dug in on top of Chu Pong and on its east slope, secure in a vast tunnel network. Possessing the high ground, they look right down Moore's throat. A third regiment of Viet Cong is also reported in the area; though just where, we're not sure. So, up to three regiments against one battalion— steep odds."

Blake eyed McCowen.

"Given the size of the landing zone, only eight of Moore's sixteen Hueys could land at the same time, which turned out to be a big problem. The first lifts arrived at 1050 this morning, dropping off Moore, his command element, and one of his four companies. A second series of lifts followed and deposited most of a second company.

"Problem is that the round trip took fifty minutes to an hour. The last troops inserted didn't arrive until around 1515—barely an hour ago.

"The NVA were initially spotted moving down the east face of Chu Pong to the dry creek bed on Moore's west flank. They first engaged him shortly after noon when he had barely two companies on the ground defending the LZ. At first, they attacked in probes of five to ten men, but later in company-size units, 100 to 150. Their movements are concealed by thick vegetation and elephant grass, and they've been able to get to within meters of Moore's perimeter without detection. He's had airstrike support, and it's made a lot of difference."

Blake paused to allow the thundering of helicopters to dissipate overhead.

"The NVA are targeting the incoming and outgoing choppers and have shot down at least two of his Hueys. Some of our guys never made it off the choppers. It's likely that all of the choppers took hits."

Blake narrowed his eyes.

"A lot of friendly casualties—Moore estimates a third of his command. On top of that, one of his company platoons is cut off."

Blake tapped two green grease-pencil circles on the aerial photograph map.

"This big circle is Moore's battalion defensive position around the landing zone. The smaller one is his best guess for the cut-off platoon."

"Not good," McCowen murmured under his breath.

"For a fact, sir. Maybe eight bad guys to one good guy. Our job is to provide illumination when and where he wants it. Though when that might be, we don't know.

"Two artillery batteries are providing direct support, and Moore intends to use them for routine illumination. But if—I should say when—things really get hot, he'll want us on station with the big flares. And you know what that means. When he does, he'll want us pronto. His call sign is Trojan Six, and the forward air controller is Red Rider."

Blake paused.

"Major, you flew four hours this morning, and Latham's crew can do the mission if need be. In fact, I have a call into him now. But Colonel McLaughlin asked me to check with you, to see if you ..."

"Of course," McCowen interjected.

"You're sure, sir?"

"We'll be fine, Randy."

"He'll be glad to hear it, sir. And some good news. The weather tonight will be clear with light east winds. And the NVA reportedly have few, if any, anti-aircraft weapons—all or most destroyed in engagements last month."

Blake closed his folder.

"That's about it, sir. I'll keep you posted as we know more. Once the sun is down, you and your crew need to be here in the briefing room. I'll make sure we have all the coffee you can stomach."

McCowen allowed a thin smile.

*****

During the balance of daylight, McCowen briefed his loadmaster and crew chief and pre-flighted the C-123 twice, each time ignoring the unpatched holes in the plane's fuselage.

Through the evening, the crew exchanged small talk, wrote letters, read, played solitaire, ate C-rations, drank coffee or water treated with quinine, the taste masked with orange Kool-Aid. Eventually, McCowen ordered lights out, the three of them reclining fully dressed on canvas cots in a room smelling of mosquito repellant.

*****

Midnight came and went, and at 1:00 AM, Blake peeked his head in. "An update, Major McCowen. Colonel Moore reports continuous probing of his perimeter. Nothing big, but it could get that way. I trust you guys are comfy."

At 3:20 AM, McCowen awoke to bright ceiling lights and pounding on the doorframe.

"Sir, go time!" Blake shouted. "They want us now, sir!"

Ten minutes later, McCowen rolled the C-123 onto the tarmac and applied full throttle, the G-forces increasing.

He leveled off at 4000 feet and goosed the engine RPMs to the red line as the aircraft headed west. Fireworks were already visible around Chu Pong Mountain, twenty-five miles distant.

Two hundred 27-pound illumination flares lined the aircraft's cargo bay. Per standard procedure, the loadmaster and crew chief checked and rechecked the flare canisters for properly primed fuses.

Fifteen miles out, McCowen broke squelch. "Red Rider and Trojan Six, this is Smoky Bear. We're eight minutes in-bound. Can give you three hours on station or until candles gone."

"Roger, Smoky Bear," Red Rider said. "You copy, Trojan Six?"

"Affirmative," Moore said, his voice barely distinguishable above the din of small arms, automatic weapons, and mortar rounds. "Good to have you with us, Smoky Bear."

Five miles out, McCowen assessed the situation in the light from the artillery illumination rounds.

"Smoky Bear, Red Rider. Close air support is inbound, will be on station in five. Need you to light up the—"

"Smoky Bear, Trojan Six," Moore interrupted.

"Go ahead, Trojan Six," McCowen said.

"They are hitting us hard at three points on our western perimeter. At least two battalions of NVA. More streaming down the mountainside. You'll see a dry creek bed. The bad guys are west of it. Light up the east slope of Chu Pong. That's where they're coming from. You copy?"

"Copy, Trojan Six. We'll make it daylight."

Three miles out, the firefight and the silhouette of Chu Pong Mountain took on dimensions. The enemy's green tracers and Moore's red tracers crisscrossed ahead of the aircraft.

"Smoky Bear, Red Rider. Flash your landing lights. Air support is on station, birds circling. Need you to start a run ASAP."

McCowen flicked his landing lights on and off and began a sweeping turn.

"Got you, Smoky Bear," Red Rider said. "Am shutting down artillery illumination."

In the blacked-out cockpit, the plane virtually invisible from the ground, McCowen observed the last artillery illumination round winging its way earthward, its light sufficient to reveal Moore's position, the creek bed, and Chu Pong's east slope—alive with movement. He throttled back on airspeed.

"On my mark," McCowen announced over the intercom.

His crew chief opened the fuselage door, and the loadmaster stood in the doorway with the first flare.

"Three ... two ... one ... DROP!"

The loadmaster and crew chief dropped flares every three to four seconds the length of the drop line, each flare burning with two million candle power, illuminating a radius of half a mile.

McCowen banked the C-123 and circled for another run, green tracers streaking skyward.

Ping! Ping! Ping!

Incoming rounds ricocheted off the plane's metal skin.

"Small arms," McCowen said. "No punch at our altitude."

Each flare run expended five flares, each flare burning bright as day for three minutes. As McCowen flew the runs, he observed the swarm of fighters strafing and bombing the mountainside.

Flying above the fighters, the C-123 shuddered as bombs and napalm slammed the enemy-infested mountainside.

"Spot on, Smoky," Moore barked over the radio. "Don't change a thing. Keep the same line."

"Smoky Bear, Red Rider. Lots of bodies down there. Our guys are having a field day."

For two hours, McCowen and team lit up the hillside, sufficient time for the fighters to expend their ordnance.

At 6:06 AM, flares expended and the horizon brightening to the east, McCowen pressed his mic. "Red Rider, Trojan Six, this is Smoky Bear. We are out of candles. Repeat, out of candles."

"And the enemy is back in his cage," Red Rider exclaimed.

"Smoky Bear, Trojan Six." Moore's southern drawl was calm. "Fine work up there. And we are mighty grateful. In fact, you saved our bacon ... at least for the time being."

"Glad to help, sir."

"A question, Mr. Bear."
"What's that, sir?"
"What are you doing tonight?"

CHAPTER THIRTEEN

In the rearview mirror as the shuttle crossed the 7.5-mile long I-10 bridge from Spanish Fort to Mobile, McCraney glanced at Lombardo.

"Sam, WWII had to be the worst. Why don't you guys ever talk about it? Us young bucks would love to hear your stories."

Beard, McCowen, and Gossen waited for Lombardo's reply.

"TM, if we could remember, we would. Besides, what you guys faced and did in Vietnam scares the bejesus out of me. Snakes, pongee stakes, jungles, leeches. I mean, just hearing Bill's story … at least he was in the air. But you—you Marines were certifiably nuts."

McCraney chuckled. "No argument there."

"Tell me, TM," Beard said, on his feet and stretching. "What possessed you to join the Marines? And don't tell me it was *to be all you could be.*"

Gossen shook his head. "Army, John. That was an Army thing."

"The truth?" McCraney said. "I joined to stay out of jail."

Lombardo was sure he hadn't heard right.

"I was raised in Gadsden, Alabama, John. I dropped out of high school after two years and bummed around. Then, with a friend, I hitched to California. I was maybe sixteen and thinking things might be different there, being how things were for us—you know—here in the South. But things weren't. Just more expensive. I ended up working with a lot of Latinos picking fruit and vegetables and doing all kinds of odd jobs. All for minimum wage or just room and board."

"And then decided to join the Marines?" McCowen pressed.

"Not exactly. I got into a little mischief with some other pickers. Too many cervezas, and maybe a weed or two. We got hauled in to sober up. And Camp Pendleton was right there—always looking for volunteers. Marine recruiters were everywhere and made the rounds of the police stations. After sleeping it off, the cell door opens and in walks a Marine dressed for parade. He made me and another guy an offer. Said no telling what might happen if we were arraigned. But he could make it all go away if we joined the Marine team for two years."

McCowen grinned. "How could you refuse that?"

McCraney snickered. "Hell, it's a great looking uniform."

"You couldn't get me in one of those rice paddies for love or money," Beard said. "No, sir. Out in the open, not knowing who or what was behind the next dike, or being dropped in a jungle, cutoff from the world."

"You got used to it, John. You had to."

"You see a lot of action?" Lombardo asked.

"Enough. Seemed we were always going out, coming back, going out again. Out for two days to two weeks. Mostly reconnaissance stuff."

"What do you mean, reconnaissance?" Gossen asked.

"Snooping on Charlie, tracking and reporting his movements, checking things out."

"What things?"

"Trails, hooches, tunnels ... to see where they went."

Gossen wrinkled his nose. "You went down in tunnels?"

"Yeah. All us newbies had a turn as tunnel rats and point man."

Beard shifted in his seat. "I'm about to crap my pants, TM. Don't tell me that didn't mess with your head."

"Sometimes. But, like I say, you got used to it. The Viet Cong and the North Vietnamese, they loved to dig tunnels. Dug a lot of them. They lived underground. I remember one tunnel. It opened to some sort of hospital. Huge. Medical stuff, straw beds, bloody rags, photos of Ho Chi Minh."

"Anyone in it?" McCowen asked.

"Nope. Least I didn't see anyone. They tended to scoot pretty quick, sneaking out another ways. No telling. They'd hide in the tunnels during the day, come out at night. And when we came up on one, somebody checked it out, and then we did what needed doing, set charges to keep Charlie from using it again. At least for a while."

McCraney paused as though reflecting.

"But, yeah, later. After I was back in the States, it did mess with me. I hit the booze and the drugs pretty hard. Did it for a lot of years. Self-medication, right? Did all kinds of jobs to feed the habit. That didn't help and the jobs never lasted. Left California when I was twenty-five and went back home, but nothing for me there. Traveled all over the states and Mexico. Spent twenty-some years in Philadelphia and married a druggie."

McCowen shook his head.

"Yep, I was some kind of messed up. Ballooned up to 250 pounds, I did, and got stomach cancer. They took about a third of it, and I got skinny again."

"You still deal with it? The war?" Lombardo asked.

"I suppose it'll always be there. But in the lowest of lows, a fella got to me … convinced me that God and Jesus are real, and I was eff'd up big time. That God had a plan for me and could make me right. Imagine, a plan for my sorry ass. Took me a while to believe it. But ever since, I've been clean. Returned to Gadsden and married a wonderful woman who knows all my dirt. That was twelve years ago. Got me a nice home, good job, decent money. I'm blessed."

"You're amazing, TM," McCowen said. "I mean it, man. And now a deacon in your church?"

"Did you lose a lot of buddies in the war?' Gossen asked.

"Yeah. But no different than you guys."

"No, TM, not the same," Lombardo said flatly. "Sure, we lost a lot of buddies. But WWII and Vietnam—totally different. John, Bill, Joe, and me, after WWII we came back to tickertape parades, celebrations, homecomings. Didn't matter if you were Audi Murphy or a company clerk, people treated you like a hero, appreciated what you did. You guys came back screwed out the gate, called baby killers and worse. Made me sick how we treated you. You didn't do anything different than we did. You followed orders."

"We did, Sam. And I think most people understood the real score. Anyway, it's been a lot of years now, and I'm doing okay. The memorial wall in D.C. made a big difference for me, for a lot of us. I never cried so hard or for so long as when I first stood facing that wall. All those names, Sam. And I'm wondering, why wasn't mine one of them." McCraney cleared his throat. "The toughest thing for us Vietnam vets, and probably for the guys and gals serving now, is making sense of fighting and dying in wars we never end up winning."

CHAPTER FOURTEEN

**Vietnam—Quang Tri Province—1969
A mile south of the Demilitarized Zone**

Under the searing 100-degree midday sun, Tommy McCraney, nineteen, sat on a stump in Tiger Stripe fatigues, his face masked with camo paint. He scanned his assigned sector of the perimeter while the other five Marines in the recon team did the same. Hunkered inside a bamboo thicket, they were far from friendly forces, entirely dependent on a PRC-25 radio and its batteries and on Claymore mines set around the perimeter. Their mission—to observe enemy troop movement along a north-south trail twenty meters to the west and barely visible through the jungle thicket. Three days into the mission, the drill, as always, was to look, listen, and report, and not to engage the enemy unless first fired upon.

McCraney's face glistened with sweat. For months, he had been the team's radio man. His M-16 rifle and PRC-25 radio were propped up against a six-inch diameter bamboo shoot, his rifle on automatic, loaded with a 20-round clip, safety off.

His respiration measured, he slapped at a mosquito feeding on his face and examined the smear of blood. A never-ending battle, a thousand others poised to take its place. But better them than the snakes, rats, and other vermin that claimed the thicket home. In the diurnal swing of day and night and sun and rain, his salt-crusted jungle fatigues and green towel around his neck alternated between soaked and stiff. Another rash had grown between his legs, one he couldn't stop scratching. Still, he was thankful for a sense of smell dulled to the odors of bodies and calls of nature.

He glanced at his watch and gestured to the man next to him. The man, Sergeant Sweeney, the recon team leader, nodded.

McCraney depressed the radio mic, broke squelch, and whispered, "Patton Five, this is Blowfish One-Two. Sitrep negative." *Nothing happening.*

"Roger, Blowfish," came the reply.

McCraney closed his eyes, but only for an instant. One more month and he might actually be on the big bird headed home. It could actually happen. But he knew better than to dwell on it. Too many stories of guys being snuffed out just before their departure. Besides, he wasn't sure where home was—California where he became a Marine, or Alabama where he grew up.

The piercing screech of monkeys high in the jungle canopy set his teeth on edge. He traded glances with the other team members. It was the first he'd heard the monkeys since setting up in the thicket.

He reached for his M-16, focused on one thought—*shoot to kill.*

As the seconds ticked, his pulse slowed, and the adrenalin rush went back to where it had come from.

The first two days, they had reported more than four hundred North Vietnamese troops moving south down the trail, accompanied by almost as many laborers carrying weapons, rice, and other supplies. Groups of ten to fifteen small Asians, jabbering in the high-pitched gibberish he'd come to hate. Heading north on the trail were enemy wounded and two captured American airmen, hands tied to bamboo sticks behind their backs. He wondered what would happen to them.

A fresh flurry of shrieks rekeyed his senses.

Eyeing the triple canopy, he spied the dark specters swinging from tree to tree, headed south. Away from whatever was coming.

He caught and held Sweeny's eyes. The sergeant's finger went to his lips.

THUMP, THUMP, THUMP!

"Incoming!" Sweeney shouted.

The team members slumped low in their carefully crafted foxholes, McCraney and Sweeney in a two-man foxhole.

Mortar rounds landed just to the north, shards of shrapnel slicing through the bamboo thicket, severing limbs and everything else.

Sweeney tapped McCraney's shoulder and gestured for the mic.

"Patton Five, Blowfish One-Two. Party's over. Need extraction. Heading to pick-up zone Alpha. Repeat, heading to PZ Alpha."

More thumps, and seconds later mortar rounds landed south of the thicket.

"Got us bracketed, boys," Sweeney shouted. "Ruck up and take to the trail."

Seconds later, the six Marines were on the trail snaking south at the double-time, ignoring the protocol of five yards spacing.

Gomez, the newbie, led point, armed with a shotgun and a machete. His job, clear the trail and spot and warn of booby traps, the ingenious killing and maiming devices fashioned by a sadistic enemy: trip-wired grenades, buried cartridges, camouflaged pits with excrement-covered pongee stakes or poisonous snakes, and countless other deadly makeshifts. McCraney reasoned the trail wasn't tricked up yet. A dozen enemy soldiers had used it that morning.

Bruno followed Gomez and humped an M-60 machine gun and four long belts of ammo. Sweeney followed Bruno with a map in one hand and his M-16 in the other. McCraney followed Sweeny, close on his heels. Behind him, Whitey carried a fat-barreled grenade launcher that looked like a sawed-off shotgun, seven grenade bandoliers strapped across his chest. Skeeter pulled rear guard, armed with an M-16 and three extra belts of M-60 ammo.

Moving as fast as Gomez could clear trail, Sweeney called for the mic and broke squelch. "Patton Five, Blowfish One-Two. Clear to toast the recon site."

A minute later, a series of artillery salvos thundered and splintered what had been the team's home, a rude awakening for any new occupants.

With each step, McCraney tensed. He knew what was coming, that it was just a matter of time.

Yet, for twenty minutes they moved unmolested, McCraney certain they were being toyed with.

Then, overhead the *WOP, WOP, WOP* of an approaching Huey helicopter.

McCraney glanced skyward, unable to see anything through the jungle canopy.

The sound got louder.

"Blowfish One-Two, Charlie One-Zero, Where the hell are you?" the Huey pilot asked.

McCraney handed Sweeney the mic and pulled the pin on a smoke grenade, tossing it a few yards off the trail.

"Charlie One-Zero, Blowfish One-Two, popping smoke," Sweeney said. "Confirm."

McCraney watched the colored smoke billow up through the jungle canopy.

"Got yellow smoke, Blowfish One-Two. Be advised, Mayflower Eight is en route to Alpha, and two Cobra gunships are inbound."

"Very bueno," Sweeney quipped. "We can't see crap down here. How about you?"

"Negative. Without the smoke, we wouldn't have a clue."

WHOOSH! WHOOSH!

McCraney and the others kissed the ground at the sound of the rocket propelled grenades.

"Charlie One-Zero," Sweeney said, "got incoming from the east!"

Two RPGs exploded meters in front of them. Seconds later, two more detonated behind them.

High-pitched Vietnamese voices rang out from the jungle.

"Return fire!" Sweeney barked. "Return fire!"

McCraney's ears rang from the din of weapons, Chicom grenades, and rockets.

Bruno, crouched behind a tree, expended two belts of M-60 ammunition. Behind another tree, Whitey played peek-a-boo with his grenade launcher, launching a grenade with each peek. Skeeter and Gomez fired short M-16 bursts at real and imagined targets.

Hunkered with McCraney in a swale, Sweeny grabbed the mic. "Charlie One-Zero, we're pinned down. Repeat, pinned down!"

"Hang tight, Blowfish. Cobras in sight," Charlie One-Zero replied. "FYI, we have an engine light and smoke and have to head back to base. Good luck, guys."

McCraney heard the approaching gunships.

"Blowfish One-Two, this is Viper Two-One," one of the Cobra pilots announced. "Me and my wingman have your yellow smoke. Understand the bad guys are to the east. Affirmative?"

McCraney fired a burst at movement in the thicket and tossed a hand grenade.

"Affirmative," Sweeny shouted. "To the East. And close. Maybe thirty yards."

"Roger. The salad's thick down there. We'll chop it up a bit. Let us know how we're doing."

McCraney caught a glimpse of one of the gunships through a hole in the canopy. Friendly rockets and rounds from miniguns pierced the canopy, kicking up geysers of debris and smoke.

Seconds later, the Cobras delivered a second salvo.

Then, it was over. The enemy dispersed.

Whitey took an AK-47 round in the right thigh. A clean shot. A piece of shrapnel lacerated Bruno's left arm. Skeeter patched them both, and the team moved on, the Cobras circling overhead.

Ten minutes later, the Cobra team leader announced they had to split for fuel and that Mayflower Eight, a CH-46 Sea Knight, was inbound to Alpha.

Minutes later Blowfish received the Sea Knight's call.

"Blowfish One-Two, Mayflower Eight. Fifteen minutes to Alpha. How about you?"

Sweeny studied his map. "Roger, Mayflower. About the same."

Twenty minutes later, the recon team arrived at PZ Alpha, a clearing roughly one hundred feet in diameter surrounded by tall elephant grass, scrub vegetation, and a few trees defoliated with Agent Orange. The twin-engine tandem-rotor Sea Knight circled high above.

McCraney popped smoke as Bruno strafed the PZ perimeter with his M-60.

"Blowfish One-Two, Mayflower Eight. Have green smoke. Let's be quick about it. We're a juicy target."

Minutes later, the recon team was aboard the Sea Knight, the rear ramp closing.

As the bird lifted off, TM, Sweeney, and Skeeter sat strapped in web seats on one side of the bird; Bruno, Whitey, and Gomez on the other. The Sea Knight door gunners sprayed machine gun fire as the bird dipped its beak and accelerated low across the clearing before climbing in a steep ascent.

At cruising altitude, the loadmaster, a white master sergeant, unstrapped himself and started handing out cans of Coke.

"Y'all done real good down there." His voice bore a deep Southern drawl. "Real good."

Making a second round, he approached McCraney with a chocolate bar.

McCraney shook his head. "No, Sarge. I just want to shake your hand."

The master sergeant grinned and extended his hand.

McCraney took it and shook it firmly. "Just wanted you and the crew to know that we love you guys. Amazing how you keep snatching our ass out of the fire. Every time, Sarge. You never fail us."

The others nodded, toasting with Coke cans.

McCraney winked at the sergeant. "If it wasn't for these guys, I'd plant a big fat one on you."

Laughter filled the Sea Knight.

On final approach into base camp, McCraney turned to Sweeney. "What do you think, Sarge? Just another day at the office?"

Sweeny smiled thinly, "Yeah, TM. It was. And I don't know about you, but I could use a cold one about now."

CHAPTER FIFTEEN

After traversing the bridge from Spanish Fort to Mobile, passing through the city, and crossing into Mississippi, the shuttle pulled into the Mississippi welcome center for a pit stop.

"In thirty minutes, we should be in Biloxi at a gaming table," Beard told Gossen as they stood at urinals. "You a gambler?"

"I covered your bet, didn't I?"

Beard chortled. "Maybe you can win it back on the slots."

Back on the road, a sense of anticipation permeated the shuttle. As it approached the exit for the gaming venues, Beard was suddenly on his feet. "TM, you need to slow down. You're going to miss the exit."

When the exit passed, Beard turned to a grinning Lombardo.

On his feet, Gossen extended his hand, palm up, and Beard dug into his pocket.

Still on his feet, Gossen pointed to the front of the shuttle. "TM and I are the only citizen soldiers here, right? The rest of you are lifers. He and I did our time, got out, and moved on. So, how is it we're the only ones dealing with PTSD, though in my time it was called battle fatigue or combat stress."

Lombardo gave Gossen a look. "You, too? You're about as chill as they come, Joe."

"It was a long time ago, Sam."

"So, out with it," McCraney said. "What's your story?"

"Yeah. Let's hear it, ball turret gunner," Lombardo said.

"All right. To begin with, while not an orphan like John, I was as good as orphaned at birth. Abandoned, I was adopted at the hospital. I had good parents, a normal childhood, and grew up with two sisters and a brother, all younger, mom and dad obviously figuring it out. We lived in Chicago and later Arizona. I played sports, did decent in school, broke a few of the rules, and tasted the paddle.

"When I was seventeen and had finished my junior year in high school, I wanted in the service and in the war. Like everybody else. My father wanted me to wait but finally agreed to drive me to the Army Air Corps recruiter. There was a program going where you could enroll as a flight cadet, which I did. Had I graduated, I would have been an officer and likely a lifer. But the program was shut down and I was discharged. I then joined as an enlisted man and was trained as an aircraft gunner, going on to train other gunners, then sent to Italy as a replacement in '43.

"I did my time and was shipped home close to the end of the war. We were sniffed by a German U-boat all the way back. Why it didn't attack, I'll never know. Still blows my mind."

"I worked awhile for my dad in the meat packing business, met and married Johanna in '47, and we had five kids, four boys and Gretchen, who you've all met and who takes care of us now. My real career was 33 years with the Arizona Public Service."

"Doing what?" Beard asked.

"Remember Glen Campbell, his song, *Wichita Lineman?*"

"Sure," McCowen said. "A great song."

"That was me. In the cold, the snow, the heat, pouring rain, whatever. Didn't matter, people needed power, and I ran line crews for a lot of years and finished up a general foreman. During and after that, life-wise, I was the scoutmaster for my kids and grandkids. Did it for 36 years. You learn a lot about kids in the Scouts as they learn to do life honorably."

"Can I quote that?" Beard quipped.

"But that has nothing to do with PTSD," McCraney said.

"No, it doesn't. For me, what I dealt with was all about sleep. Not getting enough of it. In the war I was in a B-17 heavy bomber group. Like Sam said, a ball turret gunner. After the war, I couldn't stop dreaming about it, about being on another mission and … stuff happening. I kept having these dreams and started drinking heavily. Lost weight when I didn't have any to lose. It changed me, screwed up my personality. Before, I was always the happy-go-lucky guy, a cut up. But the war changed all that."

"You were in the thick of it, weren't you?" Beard said.

"Yeah, we were. During my time, we lost twenty-six engines and six wings."

Lombardo's eyes were saucers.

"I don't remember a mission when we didn't have aircraft damage. Once, we limped back losing all four engines, one by one, the last one crapping out on a forced landing. But the amazing thing, we never lost a man. Lord, how we defied the odds."

"Dude, that would give me nightmares, too," McCraney said. "So, how did you get over it?"

"It's been so long ago, I can't really remember. Only that I talked to a lot of shrinks and ate a lot of food. And finally just … got over it."

McCraney's phone rang.

On his feet, Lombardo put a finger to his lips, the phone to his ear. "Hey, Edith. Right. He did? Okay. Anything else? Thanks, girl, and good work. Let me know when things change."

"What's up?" Beard asked.

"Johanna found Joe's cellphone." Lombardo shot Gossen a look. "In your sock drawer?"

CHAPTER SIXTEEN

European Theater—March 1945
An Airfield near Foggia, Italy

Joe Gossen, eighteen and a staff sergeant, approached the four-engine taildragger B-17 Flying Fortress. The heavy bomber boasted red bawdy lips and the words "Hot Momma" on both sides of the cockpit. Called a "Fort," it was part of the 20th Bombardment Squadron, 2nd Bomb Group, 5th Bomb Wing, 15th Air Force, and was crewed by ten men.

He inspected his miniature home for the last seven months, the ball turret protruding from the bottom of the plane just behind its massive wings, the flak damage around the "bubble" only partially patched.

"Joe!" a man shouted, heading for another B-17. "Joe Gossen!"

Gossen turned. "Hey, Smitty! You're back. How's the leg?"

"Apparently good enough." Smith, a buck sergeant, noticed Gossen's sleeve. "You got your stripes back."

"Yeah. Maybe I can keep them this time. So, how many you got left?"

Smith held up three fingers. "Can you believe it? Two months in the hospital, the war almost over, and they send me back for three lousy missions. But after that, it's back to Jersey for me."

"Don't say it, Smitty."

"I know. How about you, Joe? You gotta have your thirty-five."

Gossen scowled. "That and another twenty-one."

"What? You looking for more medals?"

"Lazzaro still owes me three-hundred bucks."

"Lazzaro's a loser, Joe. He'll never make good."

"Yeah. And I obviously have the brain of a brick because I thought maybe he would. Anyway, after this one, you won't see me around."

Smith glanced at the cloudless sky. "So, all the way to Berlin from the boot of Italy."

"Almost," Gossen said. "Berlin is another 50 miles north of the refinery. But, yeah, once we drop our eggs, we might get a glimpse, if only a quick one. But we won't be wasting time. After seven hours, we'll be landing on fumes."

"Yeah. But think of it, Joe. Berlin. Hitler's hometown. What a story for back home."

Gossen knew better than to think of home.

A minute later, the airfield swarmed with flight crews.

Gossen spotted his nine other crewmates, including the aircraft commander, Major Don Benton.

Benton approached Gossen. "So, this is it, Joe?"

Gossen saluted. "Yes, sir. If you can get me back alive."

"I'll do my best."

Despite knowing Benton hadn't lost a plane or a man since taking command of the squadron, Gossen knew the odds. Less than one in ten crewmembers finished a tour unscathed, and he was almost done with two. Just after joining the squadron, an entire squadron in another bomb group had failed to return. Six planes—sixty men gone.

That he'd been crazy lucky so far was of no comfort. He'd played craps. He knew if you roll the dice long enough, you come up snake eyes.

Donning his leather fleece-lined flight suit, leather cap with wool earflaps, and thickly lined leather gloves, he climbed aboard the Fort and made his way back inside the fuselage to huddle with three other gunners between the bomb bay and the floor hatch to the ball turret. He had trained the other gunners, and they had proven themselves.

Sniffing the tail of the B-17 in front of him, Benton reached the runway. A minute later, he lifted the bird off the ground in a slow climb to 10,000 feet, taking his place at the head of the squadron.

Forward in the fuselage, Benton and his co-pilot, as well as the bombardier, navigator, flight engineer, and radio operator went about their business.

North of the Adriatic, the bombardier slipped down inside the plexiglass nose bubble below the cockpit. His principal duty, other than operating the bomb bay, was to operate the new Norden bombsight and man the chin machine guns. As the other gunners took their positions, Gossen opened the floor hatch and eased his five-foot-six, 125-pound frame inside the ball turret, only thin aluminum and plexiglass separating him from the earth below.

"Enjoy your last ride, Joe," Lenny Hines, the flight engineer, quipped as he closed the hatch.

In the glass bubble, Gossen tested the hydraulics of the swivel seat and the movement of twin 50-caliber machine guns charged with 1450 rounds, taking the guns through their paces, clutching the machine gun grips with gloved fingers—right to left, left to right, up and down—repeating the movements.

Satisfied, he settled in, watched the world pass below, and waited for the inevitable.

Luck of the draw, they were flying middle of the pack in a herd of more than five-hundred bombers from multiple bomber groups and wings, each group flying in box formation, mostly B-17s, but some B-24s in the bottom of the formation. The mass of airpower extended more than 50 miles in length and 5 miles in width.

Fighter escorts joined them north of the Adriatic Sea where the formation climbed to bombing altitudes of 24,000 to 30,000 feet. He was pleased to see the Red Tail P-51 Mustangs among the escorts —the black pilots from Tuskegee, Alabama. They had escorted the bombers for several months and had shown their mettle. They would hang with the herd to the target and back.

Every ten to fifteen minutes, he again worked the ball turret through its paces.

Already on sixty percent oxygen, the plane unpressurized, Gossen felt the numbing chill that accompanied every mission. Temperatures between 40 and 60 degrees below zero. With the forefinger of his glove, he removed ice crystals from inside his mask, frustrated that the supposedly repaired heating element across his left knee pad was shorting out again, each short producing a sort of bee sting.

Off and on he prayed. Mostly one-liners with no amens. *Protect us, God, please. Keep us safe, Father. Just one more mission, God. Be merciful. Hail Mary, full of grace, don't let us lose a man. Shield us with your hedge of protection. Forgive me, God, for being so stupid for a lousy three hundred dollars. Lord. I know you'll deal with Lazzaro, but how do I forgive that dirt bag? Please, God, let me see Phoenix again. Get me back home, God, and I'll do whatever you want. Anything. I swear it. Anything you want. Just get me to Phoenix where it's warm. And, Lord … take away my fear. Give me courage to do what I have to do. I know they're coming. I know they're—*

And there they were.

First specks in the sky, then a swarm of predatory birds, targeting the top and bottom of the herd and the tail-end Charlies. German fighters playing cat and mouse with the Red Tails, attacking from all directions, preferring the head-on gambit, firing continuously while playing chicken with the stacked bombers, knowing they would take out a few.

"Two bogies, twelve o'clock," Benton announced coolly.

Gossen heard bursts from the Fort's forward guns, then from the upper turret gunner, waist gunners, and tail gunner.

The red 50-caliber tracers from the Fort's thirteen machine guns seemed to fly in all directions inside the box formation.

On the intercom, Gossen and the other gunners talked over one another, shouting what was coming and from where.

Gossen spotted a bogey coming from ten o'clock low and fired a continuous burst. He kept firing until black smoke trailed from the aircraft. As it passed beneath him, he saw a Red Tail in pursuit, spewing red flashes from its wing guns.

"Chalk one for the good guys," he said to himself.

Then—as rapidly as they appeared—the German fighters broke off to refuel, rearm, and to await the Allies' trip home.

The on-again, off-again enemy fighter attacks continued until after nearly three hours of flight time the massive bomber formation turned onto the target line, the last of the German fighters breaking off to let the anti-aircraft ground crews do their worst.

Benton broke squelch. "Everybody on hundred percent oxygen. Bombardier, get ready."

As Benton spoke, puffs of white and black appeared in the blue sky, each blemish radiating jagged shrapnel in every direction. Soon the sky was full of them—the flak alley that attended every mission.

A moment later, Benton announced, "Bombardier, your plane."

Gossen winced as a flash of brilliant orange and black marked where a bomber had been, fragments of the plane falling through the formation. Ahead of him, another bomber trailed smoke from a starboard engine.

"Okay, on my count," came the bombardier's Norwegian lilt.

As the bomb bay doors opened, Gossen glanced at what lay below—refinery works, distillation towers, massive crude oil tanks, refined oil tanks, and a maze of pipelines and distribution rail lines. A second engine on the plane in front of them spewed fire. In the seconds that followed, he counted chutes. One ... two ... three ... four. Then the plane entered the death spin that would trap the others inside.

He had never seen more than six chutes emerge from a plane so wounded, and he had never heard of a ball-turret gunner making it out alive unless the plane was purposely being ditched for lack of fuel or mechanical reasons.

"Bombs away," piped the bombardier.

As the Fort's twenty 250-pound incendiary bombs sailed earthward, joining the other streams of bombs, a large piece of shrapnel slammed into the Fort's aluminum skin. Gossen's spine spasmed as the plane jerked hard to starboard.

"Holy moly!" exclaimed the waist gunner, feet above Gossen. "Got us a hole the size of a watermelon."

Responsible for assessing the bomb strike, Gossen focused solely on the bombs until they disappeared into the conflagrations and billowing black smoke encasing the refinery.

"Bulls eye," Gossen announced to a round of cheers.

Then, it was over.

The surviving bombers reformed and made a sweeping left turn that would take them on a southerly heading.

Gossen glimpsed to the north. Nothing but clouds.

✳✳✳✳✳

Three and a half hours later, the surviving bombers returned to Foggia. Exhausted, his adrenalin spent, on the return flight Gossen figured they lost three or four more bombers.

By his count, about twenty-four didn't make it.

On the ground, outside of the plane, Gossen and the rest of the crew huddled around Benton, who put a hand on Gossen's shoulder. "Apparently God wants you to go home, Joe. We're all going to miss you."

Gossen couldn't stop grinning. "Yes, sir. Thank you, sir. I can't believe it, sir. Fifty-seven missions. Wow! And I'm still here. Still alive. You guys are the greatest ... I'll be praying for you. After the war, if any of you get to Phoenix, you look me up. I'll be the only Gossen in the phone book, and I'll have cold beer in the fridge. Promise."

Benton slapped Gossen on the back. "Count on it, Joe. But for now, I've got a case of not too warm Peroni in my quarters. After we remember those we lost today, we're going to celebrate your departure."

"Hey, Joe," a man shouted, jogging towards Gossen.

Gossen turned to see Smitty holding up two fingers.

CHAPTER SEVENTEEN

As the shuttle passed the exit for the NASA Stennis Space Center on the west side of Mississippi, Lombardo mused, "I'm puzzled, guys. Edith hasn't left Veronica's hip since they discovered the shuttle missing, and she hasn't reported anyone one seeing the shuttle. Given our border encounter with the Highway Patrol, I find that strange. I don't know ..."

McCowen gave it some thought. "Could be the timing, Sam. A changing of the guard. Night shift to day shift, whatever those troopers worked. If they had already clocked out, who would know?"

Lombardo nodded, unconvinced. "That's possible. And it really doesn't matter, does it? Our day in the sun is just beginning."

*****

As McCraney descended the bridge that arched high over the Pearl River, Lombardo eyed the welcome sign to Louisiana with its fleur-de-lis.

At the I-10 and I-12 split, he told McCraney to take I-10 towards Slidell.

Beard shot Gossen his impish grin and rubbed his thumb and forefinger together. "Wrong once, but not twice, Joe. Another wager where we're going?"

Gossen rolled his eyes.

"Another fiver," Beard teased.

"Why not. I'm playing with your money. But only if you tell me where we're going."

"Fair enough." Beard waved Gossen over and whispered in his ear.

Lombardo observed the exchange without expression.

"Better gas up in Slidell," Lombardo told McCraney. "I'll pay."

Minutes later, McCraney exited and pulled into a convenience store fueling market.

"A couple of twenties should do it," Lombardo said. "And just regular gas."

Lombardo and Beard headed inside to the restroom, followed by Gossen and McCowen.

Inside, McCowen walked the snack aisle and picked up a bag of cashews and a Hershey bar. When the store bell rang, he noticed a black kid entering, wearing an oversized hoodie and baggy pants.

The kid eased past him, deftly snatching stuff from the aisle shelves and shoving it into the pockets of his hoodie and pants. After swinging by the drink coolers, he headed for the door, finding it blocked by McCowen.

"Hey, mister, what gives? Move out of the way."

McCowen didn't budge.

Lombardo returned from the restroom.

"What you doing, man? Let me by."

"Your hoodie and your baggy pants, they hold a lot, don't they, son?" McCowen's words were measured.

"What you talkin', mister?"

"I saw what you did, son."

"You didn't see nothin', mister. And I ain't hardly your son."

"How old are you?"

"Old enough to mess you up, pops."

McCowen couldn't help smiling. "You going to mess me up? A 93-year-old man? Now that would be a feather in your cap."

"Why you messing with me, man? I ain't done nothin to you."

"How old are you?" McCowen repeated, leaning on his cane.

"Fifteen. What's it to you?"

"Twelve, maybe thirteen. Not fifteen. In your pockets, you got, what—some donuts, a pint of milk, a bag of Fritos, Milky Way bars?"

"What's with you man?"

Observing the exchange, Lombardo gave McCowen a what-the-hell-are-you-doing look.

"You take that stuff without paying and it's stealing," McCowen said. "But I expect you already know that."

"Look, man, you better get out of my face … or I'll have to do you up."

"Do me up? And just what does that mean?"

"In my pocket, I got what I need to do you up, pops. So, you best not push me."

Beard appeared from the restroom to see the attendant behind the counter gesturing frantically for McCowen to let it go.

"I get it," McCowen said. "You're a tough guy. But why don't you just pay for it? Couldn't be more than a few bucks. This some sort of gang thing?"

The kid puffed up and clenched his fists, then suddenly deflated. "Look, pops. I ain't no gang man … and I don't steal, unless I have to. I … got no money." The kid stared at the floor. "I ain't ate nothin all day. Yesterday neither."

"You got parents?"

"My mom. But she's gone. Been five days now. Said it would be two. They ain't nothing to eat."

"You don't have a knife, do you?"

"How you know that?"

McCowen pulled out his wallet and extracted a bill. "Here."

The kid inspected the greenback, his eyes widening.

"For real?"

"You pay the man for what you have and what else you want. With fifty dollars, you should have some left over."

The kid shook his head. "Why you do this?"

Lombardo and the attendant exchanged glances.

"Why?" the boy repeated.

"Because I can. And because when I was your age, I was hungry. A lot of times I was hungry. Maybe hungrier than you."

"But this … this don't make sense, man …" The kid fumbled for words. "I mean … what you want from me?"

"I want you to listen."

McCraney appeared in the doorway.

"I don't know what your deal is, son," McCowen said. "And you'll never see me again. But hear this. God is real and he loves you. All the time. When you're hungry and when you're fat and happy. When you're good and when you're bad. You know that?"

The kid exhaled confusion. "Maybe … my mom takes me to church … on Christmas and Easter."

"You like going?"

"I suppose. My mom, she sings the songs and sometimes … sometimes she cries. Whispers things … to God, I guess."

"We got to go, Bill," Lombardo insisted in a low tone.

In shock, Beard, McCowen, Gossen, and McCraney looked on.

McCowen put a hand on the boy's shoulder. "You can talk to him, too."

CHAPTER EIGHTEEN

After the incident in the convenience store, Lombardo couldn't stop staring at McCowen who placidly looked out the window as if nothing had happened.

After traversing the five-mile-long twin-span bridge across Lake Pontchartrain to New Orleans, he instructed McCraney to continue toward the French Quarter on I-10, Beard shooting Gossen a thumbs up.

When the shuttle failed to slow down for the French Quarter exit, Beard, exasperated, broke the silence. "TM, you're going to miss the dang exit."

The exit passed and, off Gossen's look, Beard dug in his wallet again.

"Take exit 12B," Lombardo told McCraney. "Follow US 90 West to Calliope, then make a left on St. Charles."

At Harmony Circle, Lombardo told McCraney to turn right on Andrew Higgins Boulevard and then right on Magazine.

Lombardo stood up in the aisle, his arms wide. "We're here, guys!!"

He pointed to a man in a WWII Museum shirt and ball cap standing outside the massive museum structure. A woman, similarly dressed, stood beside him.

"Pull up to the curb, TM."

"Hey, Sam, great to see you again," the man said, "Let's get you inside. Shelly will park the shuttle and meet you right here when we're done."

Beard, McCowen, and Gossen in their vintage flight jackets followed the man inside the Louisiana Memorial Pavilion, Lombardo and McCraney following. Inside, the man passed out tickets and pins to be worn on their collars.

"Men, this is Luke Matthews," Lombardo said, introducing the man. "He's the youngest son of Mark Matthews, a member of my platoon in WWII. He's a museum volunteer.

"It's a real honor to meet you guys," Matthews said. "Sam's told me a bit about each of you, so I could judge our time together. And it's my understanding that only Sam and Colonel McCowen have been here before. Colonel McCowen, I believe you were here for a recorded interview. Is that right, sir?"

"I was, Luke. My son brought me a few years ago."

"And Colonel Beard, sir, I understand you flew B-25s in the war, and in both theaters, European and Pacific. Can that be right?"

Beard nodded. "I'm afraid so."

"And you, Mr. Gossen. You were a ball turret gunner on a Flying Fortress flying out of Italy?"

Gossen glanced at Lombardo and smiled. "You've been well briefed, Luke."

"Not entirely," Matthews said, looking at McCraney.

"This is TM, Luke," Lombardo said." He's our driver and a fellow Crispy Warrior. A Marine who did his time in Vietnam."

Matthews extended his hand. "That was my time, too, TM. With the 101st Airborne Division. No jumping, just combat assaults in Hueys."

McCraney smiled. "Yeah. I know something about that."

"Colonel McCowen, Sam told me you're the baby of the group, only 18 in the last year of the war and an aircraft gunner in Italy."

McCowen nodded. "I'm that guy."

"Like Sam said, he was my dad's platoon leader in the war. When he called last night to say you were coming and asked if I would give you a tour, how could I refuse?"

Matthews winked at Lombardo.

"Truth is, I wouldn't be here if it wasn't for Sam. He literally saved my dad's life in the Battle of the Bulge and probably afterwards."

Lombardo waved him off.

Matthews signaled to an attendant who produced a wheelchair. "For you, Colonel McCowen, that is, unless you refuse it."

McCowen beamed. "No, I'm not proud. Thank you."

"Sam said I have two and a half hours for the tour and then you're back on the road. A comprehensive tour deserves at least a day, more if you have the kind of history you do. So, you'll be drinking from a firehose.

"First a two-minute history if I may. In WWI, 20 million people died, and the American battle death toll was less than 54,000. By comparison, in WWII 40 to 80 million people died, depending on whose numbers you use, with the American death toll nearly 300,000.

"The museum is a private, non-profit institution, originally called the National D-Day Museum, the idea of historian and author Stephen Ambrose who wrote *D-Day* in 1994, a factual account of the invasion. The museum opened on June 6, 2000, the 56th anniversary of D-Day. Originally, it focused on the amphibious landings at Normandy and highlighted the importance of the wooden shallow-draft Higgins boats made in New Orleans by Higgins Industries. Almost 24,000 were produced during the war. Since 2000, the campus has been expanded, and much more has been added to where the scope of the museum is the entire war, both the European and Pacific theaters. And more's to come.

"In 2013, the US Freedom Pavilion, known as the Boeing Center, was opened, and it's guaranteed to make your eyes pop, especially for Colonels Beard and McCowen and Staff Sergeant Gossen. At a hundred feet tall, it's the museum's tallest building and features six different WWII aircraft suspended from the ceiling.

"In late 2014, the "Road to Berlin" European Theater Exhibition was opened in the Campaigns of Courage Pavilion. On the floor above, the "Road to Tokyo" Pacific Theater Exhibition was opened in 2015. These are sure to bring back memories.

"But first, we'll see the 4-D film, *Beyond All Boundaries*. It was produced and narrated by Tom Hanks and sets everything up. Mr. Hanks has been a huge supporter of the museum, having produced *Band of Brothers* and *The Pacific*, and, coming soon, *Masters of the Air*." Matthews smiled. "And, of course, he played the lead in *Forrest Gump*.

"Then we'll do the Campaigns of Courage exhibitions and finish with the aircraft pavilion. Once done, Shelly will have box lunches and soft drinks and waters in the shuttle for your ride back to Florida.

"Sound like a plan?"

CHAPTER NINETEEN

Seated in the museum's IMAX theater, on what they would find to be vibrating seats, the escapees listened to Tom Hanks as he narrated *Beyond All Boundaries*. The 45-minute film featured first-hand narrated war accounts, mesmerizing historical video footage of the conflict in Europe and the Pacific, and computer-generated graphics and visual effects that gave life to the war and the circumstances on the home front.

After exiting the movie, a young boy in an Army T-shirt stained with mustard approached Lombardo.

"Were you there, mister, in the war?"

Lombardo was taken by the boy's expression of awe. "I was."

"Was it really like that?"

Lombardo wondered at the question. "Yes, young man. It was."

"Wow! That must have been so cool, so exciting."

Lombardo considered the boy and his innocence. "How old are you?"

"Seven, but almost eight. Close to seven and a half."

Lombardo smiled. "Yeah. It was exciting."

******

After a short restroom break, Matthews led the group to the "Road to Berlin" European Theater Exhibition and summarized what they would be seeing. At the exhibition entrance, the cast of international players and sides they chose were set forth. An animated map illustrated the ominous expansion of Nazi and Fascist control over

Europe and North Africa, save for the United Kingdom and neutral Switzerland.

Having just read *Milestones to Disaster*, the first volume of a five volume series penned by Winston Churchill entitled *The Second World War*, Lombardo focused with fresh interest on the Museum's treatment of events and personalities that propelled a defeated Germany after WWI to wage a much more destructive and global conflict only two decades later. Churchill had lucidly connected the many dots of unfounded optimism and strangling pacifism that enabled uncontested rejuvenation and rearming of a former enemy, and America's lethargy and isolationism that fueled the kindling of a perfect fire.

They entered the main exhibition hall on a wide winding concrete path that proceeded through spotlighted displays, maps, news clippings, shadow boxes filled with artifacts, weaponry, videos, newsreels, black and white photographs, scenes and settings of land battles, images of aerial combat, all of which testified to the global extent of the war.

The exhibition focused particularly on America's belated commitment to the Allied cause, its military maturation from North Africa to Sicily and Italy, to the D-day landings at Normandy, to the Nazi Ardennes counter-offensive, to the crossing of the Rhine into Germany's heartland, to Mussolini's assassination and Hitler's suicide, to the unconditional surrender of the European Axis powers, to the jubilation of VE-Day, to tickertape parades, and to negotiated Allied occupation of Germany that foreshadowed the coming Cold War with the Soviet Union.

While in the exhibition room featuring the Africa campaign, Matthews approached Beard. "Colonel Beard, sir, you flew in North Africa?"

"I did. Arrived in December of '42. Flew B-25s as a co-pilot until I bargained for my own plane."

"Bargained?" Matthews repeated.

"I had proven myself as a pilot, and after a mission when we took a German 88 in the nose, I was given a choice because of something I did. A Silver Star or command of my own aircraft. I chose my own aircraft, and because I could read a map and navigate terrain, I was soon the lead pilot for my squadron. We provided close air support for the British and later the Americans against Germany's

Rommel, the Desert Fox, until the Nazis gave up Africa at Tunisia in '43. We flew mostly low altitude, a few thousand feet above the ground, searching for targets, diving on bridges, rail lines, fuel depots, infantry, artillery, tanks. No shortage of targets."

Expecting Beard to bring up being a sergeant pilot, Lombardo was surprised he didn't.

"And after North Africa?" Matthews asked.

"We followed the Nazis to Sicily and did the same thing there. That was only for a month or so. Then, we flew close air support for amphibious landings in southern Italy, moving inland with the land forces."

Matthews paused at the Battle of the Bulge exhibit, an artificial wintry snow setting with a foreboding dark forest, emotionally chilling to Lombardo despite its fiction. He flinched at the percussive sound of a German 88 howitzer, managing an embarrassed smile.

"Sam?" Matthews said. "Dad never talked much about the war. Only that it was here or somewhere close to Bastogne that you guys, just replacements a month before, were on the front lines and outmanned. He said you were on quarter rations, little ammunition, constantly engaged, expecting the worst. You remember it that way?"

Having taken in the scene, Lombardo's eyes glistened. "Like yesterday, Luke … I mean, look at this—they really nailed it. Charlie would have loved it."

"Charlie?" Matthews asked.

Lombardo didn't answer.

At a point along the walkway, there was a glass incasement containing aircraft images and paraphernalia, hundreds of Allied bombers projected on the ceiling in mass formation, and aerial combat images on peripheral walls. The visuals and sounds brought the European air war to life. Fighters climbed and dove, destroyed bridges, petroleum tanks, industrial centers. And throughout the exhibition, period commentators narrated what was happening.

Standing next to Beard, a father and young daughter watched a video of B-25s strafing a railroad yard. The girl eyed Beard's flight jacket and a flight jacket contained in a display case. She pulled on his sleeve and pointed at the jacket in the display case.

Beard nodded, his eyes moist.

The "Road to Berlin" tour took fifty minutes, and after another restroom break, Matthews steered the group to an elevator that ascended to the second floor. There, beginning in the foyer room, configured as the bridge of the USS Enterprise, he narrated the "Road to Tokyo," highlighting Japanese initial expansion into Manchuria, then throughout the Pacific and southeast Asia, including its attack on China and the United States at Pearl Harbor.

Without stopping for more than a minute or two at any one exhibit, he led the group through the whole of the exhibition, speaking to American response to Japanese aggression, its mobilization from weakness to victorious strength. He spoke to a nation united and the incredible efforts on the home front to defeat its fascist enemies.

It hadn't registered on Lombardo that Doolittle's B-25 raid on Japan's mainland occurred only five months after Pearl Harbor, and that Allied sea and air victories in the Coral Sea and at Midway just two months later put Japan on the defensive for the balance of the war.

Matthews spoke to the sequence of sea and island battles from Guadalcanal to Iwo Jima and Okinawa, and the dropping of the atomic bomb on Hiroshima and Nagasaki that forced Japan's unconditional surrender. He emphasized what military analysts had concluded—that an Allied invasion of the islands of mainland Japan would have resulted in two to four million allied casualties and extended the war for an indefinite period of time.

In an exhibit room devoted to the China Burma India (CBI) theater, Matthews allowed Beard time to soak in the multimedia summary of the campaign and the brutal treatment of the Burmese and Indochinese by the Japanese, as well as captured Allied service men and women.

"Where did you fly, John?' McCowen asked.

Beard referred to a wall map and a table schematic, pointing out his area of operation and his main entry routes and targets. He spoke to the additional assignment he volunteered for to lead twenty C-47 guerilla resupply missions, the flights not included in his third combat tour count despite having been under fire flying into and out of the sites needing resupply.

"John," McCraney muttered, "did you have some sort of a death wish?"

After a short time in a room reflecting the celebration of VJ-Day and WWII, Matthews led the group to the elevators, the "Road-to-Tokyo" tour having taken forty-five minutes.

"Well, what do you think, so far?" Matthews asked.

"In a word, incredible," Beard said. "The big screen movie was great, but the exhibitions have so much more to see and know."

McCowen agreed. "I hope my son will bring me back again. Missing almost all the war, there's so much more I want to see."

"How about you, Sam," Matthews asked.

"A lot more museum than last time, Luke. What struck me, is that so much of what we see here was in the newspapers accounts I read 75 years ago. The old newsreels, background sounds, narrations … they all took me back. No way folks today can truly understand what it was really like. But the museum at least gives them a feel."

"Are we still good to see the planes?" Gossen asked.

"You bet, Joe, That's our last stop,"

In the Boeing Center Freedom Pavilion, they craned their necks and gawked at planes suspended from the ceiling at different heights—a B-17, B-25, Red-tailed P-51 Mustang, F4 Corsair, Douglas Dauntless, and an Avenger. On the ground floor, an old Sherman tank claimed Lombardo's attention. A sign pointing to the *Tang,* America's most deadly submarine, claimed McCraney's.

Matthews wasted no time taking Beard, McCowen, and Gossen, up the elevator to a mid-height gantry for a close up view of the B-25 bomber. Without a word, Beard walked the gantry to the plane that was his home for the war. Gossen and McCowen hung back on the gantry, Gossen staring fixedly at the ball turret on the bottom of the B-17 Flying Fortress 20 feet above them.

"Colonel Beard, sir," Matthews said, "I'll take Colonel McCowen and Mr. Gossen to the top gantry for a closer look at the huge B-17. You have ten minutes. Then let's meet on the ground floor."

"Roger," replied Beard.

Exiting the elevator on the top floor, Gossen walked the highest gantry, not taking his eye off the bubble on the bottom of the B-17. McCowen followed on his scooter.

Abreast the big bomber, Gossen mused under his breath, "So many hours in that glass bubble, always thinking my luck would run out."

McCowen nodded. "But it didn't, Joe. I've heard that the average lifespan of a B-17 in WWII was ten to twelve missions."

"Don't remind me."

McCowen cracked a smile. "You used up most of your nine lives in that war."

Twenty minutes later, the Patriot House escapees were standing on the curb when Shelly arrived with the shuttle, announcing box lunches and waters, bottled tea, and soft drinks in a cooler on the back seat.

CHAPTER TWENTY

After thanking Matthews and Shelly, Lombardo checked his watch. "Load up boys. We're behind schedule. We'll head back the way we came, TM. See if you can make up some time."

As they drove from the museum enjoying muffuletta sandwiches, chips, and a Moon Pie, McCraney managed the meal as best he could. There was no banter, each man lost in his own thoughts. On the long bridge from New Orleans to Slidell, McCraney slipped behind a rabbit running at eighty-five.

After half an hour, Lombardo shuffled to the front of the shuttle. "It's too quiet in here. So, tell me ... what did you think?"

Gossen was the first to answer. "This trip, Sam ..."

"Yeah, Joe?"

"Just ... thanks."

"That's it ... thanks?"

"No, seriously, Sam, I mean it. Thank you for this trip."

Beard nodded. "Some blackjack would have been nice, but this has been great, Sam. It's certainly been one helluva mission, and it's not over yet."

McCowen cleared his throat. "Goes for me, too, Sam. Your call last night ... I was thinking you'd lost it. But the whole thing. Keeping us in the dark, wondering what you had planned. The museum was perfect. What a memory. Your young Matthews totally understood the connection. An amazing day, Sam. I'll never forget it."

Lombardo smiled dubiously. "Amazing? Weren't you almost knifed."

McCowen grinned. "Maybe that was the best part, Sam. I can't remember being so alive."

Lombardo beamed. "There you go." He pointed to the rear of the shuttle. "A piece of each of us is back in that museum." He thumped McCraney on the shoulder. "You, too, TM. Seeing the Burma jungles and what Merrill's Marauders wormed through must have stirred your heart strings."

McCraney snickered.

"Funny," Gossen mused. "In the museum, seeing the B-17 hanging in the air, I closed my eyes. And just like that, I was inside that ball turret again. It gave me chills. So long ago. All those missions ... and me so stupid."

Lombardo chuckled. "My daughter Michele did an internet search. She said less than half a percent of us WWII vets are still alive. For comparison, she said the last Civil War soldier died at 106."

"You and John," McCraney quipped, "you relics could break that record."

"Wise-ass," Beard said, turning to Lombardo. "Is it true, Sam? What I heard about you and the Super Bowl?"

Lombardo shrugged equivocally. "Son Mark says so, but nothing final yet. They just want to recognize a few WWII vets at halftime. Before we're all gone."

McCraney gave Lombardo a toothy grin. "Damn, Sam, How cool is that? You on the field at the Super Bowl. A billion people watching. All that glitz. All those cheerleaders."

Lombardo's ears perked. "Cheerleaders?"

Crossing into Mississippi, Lombardo was again on his feet. "I've been thinking, guys."

Beard grinned. "Not again."

"Seriously, we've all lived a lot of history, right? As a result, we're now the old men we never thought we'd be ... at least, I didn't. And not only old, but ancient ... except for the kid driving this tank."

"Thank you," McCraney said.

"So, my question ... have we made a difference?"

Beard, McCowen, and Gossen exchanged glances.

"How do you mean?" Beard asked.

"Do you think your life has made a difference, John?"

"We won the war, didn't we?"

"Old news. I mean, when it's our time, will we have left the world a better place? That kind of difference."

"I think we all have, Sam." McCowen allowed. "Maybe not on some grand scale, but where and when we could. With family, friends, and in the circumstances we've lived. Not that any of us is a saint. For my part, that's why God put me here. To make a difference."

"Being a stockbroker 45 years after leaving the service, I made folks a lot of money," Beard offered glibly.

"Let me phrase it differently," Lombardo said. "Have things improved during our lifetimes, independent of what we've done?"

"Now there's the question," Gossen said. "Any of you read Orson Wells' *1984*. It came out about 1950; made a film in the '80s."

Lombardo, Beard, and McCowen said they had.

"For some reason, in my twenties, that story absolutely stopped me in my tracks. It made such an impression, I read it again. I accepted that what was in the story could happen in a communist or totalitarian state, but, lord, I never thought it could happen to us. Now, I'm not so sure. Seems *Big Brother* is all around us … started out *little brother*, but no longer."

"The red menace," Beard mused in agreement. "The film that got me was *The Manchurian Candidate*. Not that we can do anything about it. At 101, other than voting, fretting over what I can't control makes no sense. Our time has passed. Time for the next shift."

"Hobo philosophy?" queried Lombardo.

"Maybe. But what can you do when the capitol aisle is a Berlin Wall? The red and the blue don't talk to each other. One side enlisting lawyers and government agencies against the other and the people they're supposed to protect."

Lombardo nodded. "It's all about power. Thinly veiled Black Shirts all over again. We need more John Waynes and Doris Days. We need another Ronald Reagan."

"Those were good days," Gossen agreed. "Remember when we were kids? Halloween? We'd trick-or-treat without a bodyguard or any fear of weirdos. I was out hustling all the treats I could, even in the Depression, and maybe soaped a window or two when folks turned off their lights. My parents never questioned where I was or when I'd be back."

Lombardo smiled. "Yeah, I remember after we immigrated, my first Halloween. I dressed up like a cowboy, thinking how cool I looked. When I hit the streets, every other kid was a cowboy. No one loved Halloween more than I did."

"But to your question, Sam," McCowen said. "Are we in a better place? Who can honestly say we are? Not even close. Society is a trainwreck. The moral decay in the country sickens me, and it's all happened so fast. Politicians and power players think they have the authority to define right and wrong, good and bad, what's pure and perverted."

"Amen," Gossen murmured.

"The Bible is clear," McCowen said. "The Koran for that matter—men are men, and women are women. It's not a choice thing. And it's pure evil to raise kids to think they can choose what they want to be biologically. That's twisted. All I know is that Sodom and Gomorrah happened. And there's no reason to think it can't happen again. Illegal immigration, rampant drugs, human trafficking, bashing the police, trashing our cities, encouraging the homeless to be homeless, putting hardened criminals on the streets, letting looters go free, turning a blind eye to crooked politicians … I mean, how insane is that?"

McCowen's soliloquy silenced the shuttle for half an hour.

"Sam," McCraney ventured, breaking the silence, "a word from the peanut gallery?"

"Sure, TM. What is it?"

"I agree with Bill. But what goes around, comes around. Not that we'll see it, as flipped as things are. But if you believe in God, which most of us do, and I pity those that don't, you know he's going to deal with it. We just don't know when or how."

"I'm not sure I want to know," Beard said cynically.

"Who would?" McCraney agreed. "Anyway, and I could be wrong, but when you guys see me when I show up at Crackings, who do you see? A black man? An African American? Or another vet?"

Lombardo chortled. "A hungry vet."

"For a fact," McCraney said with a grin that evaporated. "Born after your war, I grew up Jim Crow, right? Everything separate-but-equal, except it wasn't. Not even close. Martin Luther King took a stand … and others did. But it was King that got it right. Peaceful protests, take the abuse—God knows there was plenty of it—but keep on, keeping on.

"Broke my heart when I heard King had been assassinated, me still in Nam. Every one of color wondered if it was over. His dream. Our dream. But it wasn't, was it? I still pinch myself at what's happened since he died."

"A lot of change," Gossen agreed.

"Like night to day, and mostly good. I can't count the number of times I've repeated King's line, *Free at last!*"

Lombardo nodded.

"But it's been a long time since King and the others did what they did, and, sure, not all that's happened since has been good, but why dwell on it now? Today's kids—black, brown, red, or white—unless poisoned by those who can't let go—have no reason to go there. History is history, especially history lived by those dead. And what they did or didn't do we learn by, right? Or should. Now, except for the pot stirrers, I don't see how we could be on more equal footing. All of us. Who is it that can't pursue their happiness, their best interest, the same as everyone else so long as they don't step on the rights of others?"

McCowen offered an amen.

McCraney slowed for flashing blue lights, a two-car wreck on the side of the road.

"And for you, Bill, poverty was your slavery, but you overcame it. For me, it was in Nam when I first really understood what was going on. My Marine buddies and me, we fought side by side. Nothing we wouldn't do for each other. And when we lost a buddy, it hurt. Didn't matter their color or background, we cried for him. We mourned for him and mourned for his family. God knows we did. It just—"

McCraney hesitated, Lombardo sensing his emotion and squeezing his shoulder. "I know, TM. Good words, brother."

"You should give up preaching, TM," quipped Beard, "and run for office."

McCraney wiped his eyes. "No way, just a deacon with a rap sheet. Like you said, John, you've done what you could, and I'm almost there. I just hope those who can, will. And if not now, soon, or it's all over."

CHAPTER TWENTY-ONE

After crossing the Perdido River into the Florida panhandle, McCraney pulled into the Florida Welcome Center, Lombardo declaring, "This is our last stop." It had been a full hour since Edith called, and he found himself continually checking his watch.

Back on the road, McCraney's phone finally rang, and Lombardo was on his feet.

"Hey, Edith. What's going on? Really?" Lombardo's eyes narrowed. "No, it's okay. I figured as much. When? Where are you? Right. Listen, I want you to find Veronica. No, I'll stay on the line. And when you find her, tell her—"

Lombardo covered his mouth, communicating in a whisper before hanging up and turning to the others.

"Gig's up, boys. Veronica knows or at least thinks we have the shuttle."

"And you want to talk to her?" Beard said, incredulous.

"I knew it, Sam," McCraney said in a resigned tone. "You do know they can trace a cellphone?"

"Not to worry, TM. Unless they do, they haven't a clue where we are."

A minute later, Veronica was on the phone, and Lombardo put her on loudspeaker, not needing to. The others winced at her high pitched rant.

When she stopped for a breath, Lombardo jumped in. "I know, Veronica. It was stupid. But it was me that was stupid. Not the others. The important thing is we're all fine and nothing's happened to the shuttle. The four of us just needed some time and space to reflect on Charlie. That's all. We'll be back for supper, the shuttle topped off and—"

Veronica interrupted with another tirade.

Lombardo held the phone arm's length. "I'm sorry … what was that, Veronica? You're breaking up … I think I'm losing you … must be a blind spot … sorry, girl."

Lombardo powered the phone off and handed it to TM. "Gentlemen, we are no longer in communication with basecamp."

Beard crossed his arms. "What happens now, Custer?"

Minutes later, Lombardo told McCraney to take the I-110 cutoff through Pensacola. Crossing the three-mile bridge to Pensacola Beach, the shuttle headed east through Gulf Breeze on Highway 98.

Gossen broke the silence. "I know we're busted, Sam. But this has been a great day. Sorry, TM."

Lombardo gazed out the shuttle window at the blur of scrub oaks, palmetto, dense shrubbery and vines that masked all that was beyond, until an opening of a hundred yards revealed the white dunes of Santa Rosa Sound. Seeing it, only for an instant, a memory was triggered.

CHAPTER TWENTY-TWO

WWII—The Ardennes, Belgium—January 1945

Samuel Lombardo, twenty-six and the platoon leader and executive officer for I Company, 394th Infantry Regiment, 99th Infantry Division, helped Charlie Geiger up and into the rear of a 2 ½ ton truck assigned to take wounded to the rear. Geiger turned and faced Lombardo, his eyes glistening, large snowflakes wafting from an overcast sky. Boots slung around his neck, he massaged one of his frostbitten feet, swollen and thickly wrapped.

Shivering in the fifteen degree temperature, Lombardo offered his hand.

Geiger shook it and hung his head. "I'm sorry, Sir."

Lombardo forced a smile. "Sorry, my ass. Tonight, you'll be in a cozy hospital, Charlie. A nurse's hands all over you. Hot chow and your feet coming back to life. Enjoy it while you can. Because they'll ship you back soon enough."

"You think?"

"Listen, Charlie, you're one of my best, and you're going to be fine. I need you. But I need you with boots on."

******

Three weeks later, after a late morning two-mile march east-northeast through the Ardennes, fewer than ten miles from the German border, Companies I, K, and L, forming one of the 394th battalions, departed a logging road and advanced through scorched woodlands. The blackened, mostly denuded forest contrasted with the white of winter.

As Lombardo's platoon trudged through shin deep snow, he took in the ironic image of two abandoned Nazi Tiger tanks. On the outside, they appeared in mint condition.

Beyond the toasted forest, a clearing loomed. Arriving at the edge of the clearing, the sun gleamed down from the zenith of a frosty blue sky. The three companies formed along the edge of the clearing— I Company on the left, K in the middle, and L on the right.

Through his binoculars, Lombardo surveyed the clearing and the hillside opposite. He estimated the clearing at a mile wide and more than a hundred yards across. The unblemished snow sparkled to the point of blinding. Beyond the clearing, the topography rose through clusters of scrub trees to a forest of firs racked by shelling.

Awaiting orders, his face stung with each blast of frigid air. He turned to the soldier next to him, Staff Sergeant Steve Rosenburg, his platoon sergeant.

Rosenburg blew warmth into woolen gloves pressed against his cheeks. "G-got to l-love it, Lieutenant," Rosenburg managed through chattering teeth.

Lombardo hiked his wool scarf up around his neck. "What I love is Jerries on the run."

A month earlier, Hitler's Panzer divisions penetrated the Allied foothold in mainland Europe, encircling the American 101st Airborne Division as well as other units in and around Bastogne. For anxious weeks, the situation looked bleak. Fog and winter storms prevented air resupply. But the weather changed, and the Allies again ruled the skies. The German second blitzkrieg through the Ardennes had stalled for lack of fuel, what some were calling the Battle of the Bulge.

The battalion commander ordered L Company forward, the other two companies to follow in echelon.

The L Company's point man stepped onto the shimmering field, his boots crunching through the crusted snow, his boots sinking out of sight. The rest of the battalion looked on passively, until the man, only five steps into the clearing, was suddenly masked in a plume of white. The accompanying explosion reverberated across the field, shrapnel skittering across the crusted snow.

When the snow settled, the men in the battalion were in defensive positions; weapons raised. L Company's point man lay in a fetal position, screaming, "My legs! Oh God, my legs!"

Two soldiers grabbed him by his field jacket and pulled him back to the edge of the clearing, a trail of red across the white canvas.

"Dammit, Sarge," Lombardo muttered. "Another Bouncing Betty."

Once triggered, the German anti-personnel mine vaulted three feet in the air and exploded. Lethal in its own right, it didn't need to be. The mangled legs and groin of a survivor would take him out of the game, along with anyone caring for him.

Hardly had the man received morphine when K Company was ordered forward, every eye on its point man. The man advanced hesitantly five yards and then another five yards before suffering the same fate.

The second man's screams mixed with the first, the first man's screams weak and soon inaudible.

Lombardo knew what was coming.

Rosenburg glowered "This is freakin suicide, Lieutenant."

"Lieutenant Lombardo," came a voice from behind him.

Lombardo turned to face Captain Gerald Morrison, I Company's commander.

"It's our turn, Lieutenant."

Lombardo nodded. It didn't matter if Rosenberg was right.

"Matthews!" Lombardo shouted.

A man stepped forward, his eyes on the ground. Lombardo put a hand on his shoulder.

"You okay, Matthews?"

Private Mark Matthews, his face drained of color, stared at Lombardo. "Sir, you saw what just happened. Please, sir, don't make me do it. My family. You've seen pictures. I just learned we have another on the way." The private's eyes welled with tears. "I'm no coward, sir. It's just—"

"No. No, you're not, Matthews," Lombardo said. "Far from it."

Lombardo glanced at L Company. Their point man lay unattended on a stretcher, a poncho draped over his body. He turned to his platoon. "Huddle up, men!"

The platoon closed in around Lombardo, none of them making eye contact.

"Listen to me. I know what you're thinking and …" Lombardo paused. "Dammit, look at me!"

Rosenburg stepped forward. "I suggest youse look at the Lieutenant and listen to what he got to say." Rosenberg's accent was Brooklyn and thick. "Or youse guys gonna wish to hell you did."

One by one, the eyes of the platoon met Lombardo's.

"I know what you're thinking," Lombardo repeated. "But it really doesn't matter, does it? We have a mission—what I laid out this morning. If we don't relieve the men cutoff beyond this clearing, we know the Jerries won't be taking any prisoners. Not with what's happened."

Lombardo pointed across the clearing. "Our buddies are over there. They are surrounded. We're their only hope."

A hawk circled high in the sky cawed. The eyes of the platoon, the company, and rest of the battalion were on Lombardo.

"So, do I have a volunteer?"

No one spoke or stepped forward.

"All right, then. I'll go first. Sergeant Rosenberg will follow me."

Rosenberg nodded, stone-faced.

"Then each squad. Maintain ten-yard separation. Each man is to step in my footsteps. Exactly in my footsteps. Understood?"

A few heads nodded.

"If anything happens to me, Sergeant Rosenberg takes my place. If something happens to him, the leader of First Squad takes his, his squad members following him ... and so on. But we are going to cross this field. We are going to finish this mission. Too many lives depend on us."

A piteous cry from the K Company point man drew attention from Lombardo. Two stretcher bearers carried the man. A third man administered a plasma transfusion.

Lombardo studied the rise beyond the clearing, his eyes drawn to the stump of a hardwood tree. Decapitated at shoulder height, it was split down the middle, the split forming a perfect V. Beyond the stump, he noticed a thin, fire-stripped pine sapling splitting the V.

Lombardo turned to the platoon. "By now, we all believe in God, don't we? Think of what he's done for us, what we've faced. None of us should be here. But we are. Crossing this field is no different. It's simple. Step in my footsteps. On the other side, we'll reform."

As Lombardo proceeded to the edge of the clearing, Rosenberg growled, "Youse all snap to it and follow me. Capisce?"

The platoon formed in a column of squads.

Lombardo felt in his fatigue pocket. In it was his rosary and the letter that others would read. He crossed himself and lifted a foot over the crusted snow. Breaking the crust, he lowered his boot through powdery snow to the frozen earth below, the top of his boot below the snow crust.

He took a second step. And a third.

With each step, he expected the worst. His feet nearly frozen, he knew he wouldn't be able to sense a mine before it sensed him. Knowing it made no sense, he walked a straight line keeping the burnt pine sapling centered in the V of the stump.

He breathed deeply, exhaling a fog of water vapor through pursed lips. Ten yards into the clearing, he paused, his chest pounding. He glanced over his shoulder. Rosenburg was advancing, his first squad leader in place to follow.

Lombardo continued, the crunching of snow the only sound in the icy stillness.

Above, a second hawk joined the first, circling, waiting.

Halfway across the clearing, he again glanced over his shoulder. Matthews and others were behind Rosenburg and his First Squad leader. The balance of the platoon was queued up at the edge of the clearing. The other I Company platoons were in line behind them. The men of K and L Companies were beginning to move.

Gradually, numbed to his fate, Lombardo's breathing relaxed. *Maybe this part of the field wasn't mined.*

A volley of long-range artillery shells shrieked overhead in the direction of their objective, the isolated American unit. A second barrage followed, answered by the crack of German 88 howitzers, the weapon Lombardo feared most.

He increased his pace.

Arriving at the far edge of the clearing, he dropped to one knee and crossed himself, then scampered up the slope. He collapsed against the split stump and gulped from his canteen.

Seconds later, Rosenburg joined him, swigging from his own canteen. "Lieutenant, youse gotta have the biggest set of balls ever."

"Easy on the water, Sarge. It's got to last."

Lombardo observed the scene across the clearing, the unbroken stream of troops.

Forty minutes later, the battalion reformed and advanced to the sound of the guns.

******

Three days later, with little sleep, scant rations, and after having relieved the besieged unit, reduced to fifty percent effectives, the battalion stood down, the contesting Germans in full retreat. Morrison notified Lombardo that the company had earned two weeks rest and recuperation, including a weekend in Paris. Rosenburg relayed the good news.

The next morning, the day sunny and the troops elated, Lombardo and the platoon marched, sang, and laughed their way rearward through snowmelt that created ankle-deep mud. The previous day had been the warmest in months. Half a mile from the snowclad clearing they'd crossed earlier, Lombardo asked for and received permission to make a detour.

Taking only Rosenburg and Matthews, Lombardo weaved through the shadowy fir forest, passing three more abandoned German tanks, parked side by side, main guns pointed west.

His heart light and his energy recovered, he breathed deep the fresh scents of forest and earth and quickened his pace. Rosenburg and Matthews struggled to keep up.

"Why ... we doing this ... Lieutenant?" Rosenburg gasped.

"I have to know, Sarge. Don't you want to know?"

Lombardo slid down a steep swale and scrambled up the other side. Sunlight shined ahead through the edge of the forest. Breaking out of the forest, Lombardo searched for the split stump.

Spotting it, he ran to it.

Rosenberg and Matthews caught up with him, all of them gawking at what lay before them.

"I freakin' don't believe it, sir," Rosenburg muttered, eyeing the snowless clearing.

"It's not possible," Matthews declared.

His mouth agape, Lombardo marveled at what he saw. The entire field was netted with rope, a mine every square meter.

EPILOGUE

Veterans Day Celebration, November 11, 2019
HarborWalk Village, Destin, Florida

A week after the return of the Patriot House escapees, forty-two Crispy Warriors in monogramed white shirts and khaki pants sat on folding chairs arranged in rows beneath an awning that covered the HarborWalk Village amphitheater stage. Most carried jackets. A banner reading *God Bless America* hung from the roofline of the stage. Across the front of the stage, a second banner read *Celebrating the Red, White, and Blue.*

McCraney climbed the stage steps and ambled to four empty front-row seats next to Igor Webb and Murray Casey.

"TM," Westy Westenbarger shouted, his voice on edge. "Where the hell are Lombardo, Beard, McCowen, and Gossen?"

"Don't you worry about them, Westy." McCraney waved to his wife in the crowd. "Trust me, they wouldn't miss this for the world."

"That's the problem, TM. I trust you. It's them I don't trust. Not after the stunt they just pulled."

McCraney let the remark pass. Lombardo had been as good as his word. No one knew of his part in the shuttle heist. Not until he parked the shuttle at the Fort Walton Beach parking lot did Lombardo tell them what he had told Veronica—that they were returning from east of Panama City, driving back from Apalachicola. How Lombardo got the shuttle back to Patriot House and what kind of reception they received, he didn't know until Gossen called the next day to tell him the facility thought it best to bury the incident and put the shuttle key in an overnight lockbox.

"This crowd is amazing," McCraney said.

Casey nodded. "A lot more than I expected."

"And perfect weather for the air show," Webb observed. "Only a few puffy clouds."

Seated fifteen feet from the stage on the front row of folding chairs, a contingent from Patriot House—Veronica, Scotty, Edith, and others of her geriatric gaggle, including Wendy—eagerly awaited the patriotic program. News teams scurried to set up camera equipment.

******

"Prop Clear!" shouted the pilot of a privately-owned vintage B-25 bomber parked at the Destin airport. The one-man ground crew pulled the chocks from the wheels.

Flipping the magneto switches, he fired the left engine and then the right, the massive propellers accelerating to an indistinct whir, the noise inside the plane deafening. The pilot turned and smiled at the man sitting next to him.

"Bring back memories, Colonel?"

Beard in his leather bomber jacket returned an impish grin.

"The rest of you guys, how about a commo check?"

"Loud and clear," reported Gossen over the intercom from the navigator bubble beneath the cockpit.

"Lima Charlie," McCowen reported from the radio room behind the pilots."

Across the bomb bay from McCowen, Lombardo barked into the intercom, "Any way you can turn down the noise?"

"Comes with the package, Colonel. Buckle up. We're off to see the wizard."

******

A family of two teenage girls and a younger boy snaked their way through the HarborWalk crowd for a better look at the stage. The boy studied the men on the stage. "Dad, those guys up there. They're really old."

A horn blared from a boat in the harbor.

A young man appeared on stage in a blue blazer, white shirt, and red slacks and wearing a blue tri-cornered hat bearing white stars trimmed in red. Handsome and muscular, he approached the lectern with a distinct limp and a mic in his hand.

"Testing. Testing. One, two, three. One, two, three. Can y'all hear me out there?"

"Got you loud and clear, sir," shouted a young black man in a Navy uniform at the back of the crowd."

"Thank you, sir! And greetings to all of you. My name is Kent Conner, and on behalf of the City of Destin and HarborWalk Village, a very warm welcome to each and every one of you on this coolish evening. Thank you for joining us for this week's patriotic program as we celebrate Veterans Day and our amazing country, the United States of America. Are we not blessed to live where we live and to have the freedoms we have?"

Deafening applause, whistles, catcalls, and chants of *U-S-A* echoed along the boardwalk of HarborWalk Village.

"On this, our big day, celebrating our one nation under God we're not alone, are we? Patriots all across the country are rejoicing in the success of the greatest experiment in human history—the American republic—two hundred and forty years and going strong. We're thankful for the founding fathers who won our independence and framed the American Constitution in which thirteen colonies became thirteen states to make up our one nation—the United States of America—a nation now boasting fifty states, proud states, as well as several territories."

More cheers followed with the waving of hundreds of small American flags passed out by the HarborWalk staff.

"And how did all this happen?" Conner asked. "It happened because of the unflinching service and sacrifice of those who stood and are standing in harm's way to safeguard our country and come to the aid of others threatened with tyranny. And what better group to honor in our own city of Destin, Florida, than our own Crispy Warriors, a veterans group spanning seven decades of faithful service to the nation."

Conner swept his hand across the stage of veterans, eliciting more cheers.

"My friends, included in the number of the Crispy Warriors are four members of the greatest generation. I'm talking about four WWII veterans. True American heroes."

Conner glanced at Westenbarger, nodding toward the empty seats.

Westenbarger shrugged sheepishly.

"Which ones are the WWII veterans," the young boy asked his father.

Conner turned back to the crowd. "But before we hear from this amazing group and how they got their name, join me in a hearty welcome for Destin's own Village Belles."

The appearance of a trio of trim come-hither young women clad in tight vintage brown skirts and jackets, triggered hoots, hollers, and catcalls.

Their faces bright, lips painted fire-engine red, hair coifed 1940s' style, topped with Army garrison caps, the trio launched into flawless harmony for a fifteen-minute medley of 1940s and 1950s military and big band songs.

Three older couples began swing dancing on the boardwalk.

Generating the loudest applause was the trio's rendition of the Andrews Sisters' 1941 *Boogie Woogie Bugle Boy*.

Upon their departure, Conner returned to the mic, flashing an enthusiastic thumbs-up.

"Now some of you may be wondering about the men behind me and the shirts they wear, shirts bearing the insignias of all our nation's armed forces."

At this, boos and sharp exchanges rang out from the back of the crowd. Five black clad and masked militants, hoisting protest signs, pushed their way through the crowd. One with a bullhorn cursed the country and the day until four Destin police officers escorted him and his cohorts off the premises to rousing cheers.

Conner flashed a broad smile. "People, could I have orchestrated that better? Freedom of speech is the cornerstone of our freedom. But not when it infringes on the peace, well-being, and rights of others."

Conner proceeded with a short history and description of the veterans' group, the origin of its name, and its visibility within the community.

Webb nudged McCraney. "I can't believe the WWII guys aren't here."

Conner raised his hands high. "So, please give a very special round of applause for Destin's own Crispy Warriors, a group of veterans representing all of the nation's armed forces and including ranks from private to general and flag officer."

It was a full minute before the applause died.

"My friends, no one appreciates freedom more than veterans and their families. They know only too well the cost of freedom. They understand that freedom isn't free. In the group on this stage are those who have fought in every armed conflict the United States has faced since, and including, World War II.

"In fact, soon you'll meet the four Crispy Warriors who served in WWII: Colonel Sam Lombardo, a platoon leader in the Battle of the Bulge; Colonel John Beard, who flew more than three combat tours, each including thirty-five combat missions; Colonel Bill McCowen, a teenage aircraft gunner and later Strategic Air Command pilot credited with the most combat missions in Air Force history; and Joe Gossen who flew 57 missions beneath the belly of a B-17 Flying Fortress."

In the ten minutes that followed, an Air Force honor guard presented the colors, and an Army staff sergeant sang the national anthem, her voice crisp, conquering all of the high notes.

Over the HarborWalk sound system, Lee Greenwood's *I'm Proud to be an American* reverberated up and down the boardwalk.

Seated near Edith, a tall, thin black man, stooped by age and wearing a weathered veteran's baseball cap stood up, supporting himself on a cane. With a shaky hand, he saluted the American flag.

Murray Casey shook his head. "Damn, if that doesn't bring tears to my eyes."

Seconds later, behind the old man, a Spanish American woman in a one-piece Marine officer's flight uniform stood and saluted the flag, surrounded by what appeared to be her family, all beaming with pride.

Soon all but those in wheelchairs were on their feet, roars of appreciation and pride greeting from those on the boardwalk.

Conner glanced at the seated veterans, many with unrestrained tears.

In the awkward silence that followed, Conner pointed to the old black man. "Thank you, sir, for your service. I only wish I could have served. That I could have done my part, as you did yours."

When the black man sat down, Edith reached over and patted his thigh. "We appreciate you, sir. More than you know."

Conner cleared his throat a second time. "Whew! Don't tell me that wasn't amazing." He turned to Igor Webb and nodded.

"Now, let's hear from a man who knows better than any of us what freedom is about. Ladies and gentlemen, please give it up for Colonel Ron, Igor, Webb, a man shot down in the Vietnam War who spent six years of his life in North Vietnamese prison camps."

Five minutes later, having finished a spellbinding narrative of ejecting from an F-4 Phantom over North Vietnam, his incarceration in Hanoi, the bond he shared with other POWs, and the genesis of his nickname, Igor, Webb received a two-minute ovation. During the ovation, he repeatedly pointed to the other men on the stage, clapping for them.

Conner glanced with narrowed eyes from Westenbarger to the empty seats, Westenbarger again shrugging.

A minute later, the roar of engines was heard, a flight of six single-engine World War II T-6 aircraft in perfect formation appearing from the west, their piston engines growling menacingly. Once over the harbor, they broke formation and soared in every direction, trailing smoke, engines screaming, rising and diving as if in aerial combat.

******

Minutes later, after departing to the northwest out of the Destin airport and climbing to two thousand feet, the pilot of the B-25 announced, "We'll come in from the west, gentlemen. Mr. Beard, why don't you take the controls and turn to a heading of one-eight-zero. Once we're over the coast, turn to a heading of zero-niner-zero."

"With pleasure, sir," Beard said.

Lombardo marveled at how smoothly Beard handled the aircraft.

Having reached the coast, Beard announced, "Zero-niner-zero, sir."

"Now, sir, take us down to one thousand feet."

Beard did as instructed.

"Excellent. Now, it's show time, gentlemen," the pilot said. "You two in the back, HarborWalk is about two minutes ahead. You'll see it off our left wing. Should be quite a crowd down there. I'll tell you when."

Lombardo nodded to McCowen as the bomb bay doors opened, revealing the earth and Gulf below.

******

As the T-6s wound up their sky show, McCraney, having received a text on his cell phone, arose and approached Conner in the wings.

As the T-6s trailed off to the east, Conner approached the lectern, an expression of disbelief on his face.

"Ladies and gentlemen, this former Marine ... what is your name, sir?"

"McCraney, sir. But most people call me TM."

Conner pointed to the empty seats. "This Marine has just informed me that the empty seats on stage, seats set up for the Crispy Warrior WWII veterans, are empty because—"

Conner's attention, indeed everyone's attention, was drawn skyward to the B-25 bomber appearing from the west, its engines roaring.

"—because," Conner added enthusiastically, pointing to the bomber, "the WWII veterans are inside that bomber. It's a B-25 bomber like the one the Doolittle squadron flew when they bombed Japan just months after Pearl Harbor. And why are they up there? Because a fellow Crispy Warrior and WWII veteran, Charlie Geiger, died two weeks ago and asked if his ashes might be spread over the Gulf."

Conner flashed a smile at the veterans on the stage and turned back to the crowd.

"Keep your eyes on the belly of that plane!"

******

Seated on opposite ends of the bomb bay as its doors opened, Lombardo and McCowen eyed the earth below, Lombardo clasping the urn containing Charlie's ashes.

"What a view, Bill," Lombardo exclaimed as Okaloosa Island passed beneath them, Choctawhatchee Bay on the left, the Gulf of Mexico on the right.

McCowen grinned from ear to ear, his camera at the ready. "I can't believe we're doing this, Sam."

"The Destin bridge is just ahead, men," the pilot announced. "On my command."

Lombardo raised the urn over the bomb bay. "No need for a parachute, Charlie."

"Now! shouted the pilot. "Drop now!"

Lombardo tipped the urn into the bomb bay as McCowen clicked his camera, again and again.

Amid the clamor and celebration below, the angular haze of gray ash descended, the ash dispersing, soon invisible against the aquamarine waters of the Gulf.

On the ground, the young boy tugged on his father's shirt and pointed skyward. "Look, Dad, up there! Where's the plane?"

East of the cheering crowds at HarborWalk Village, the B-25 bomber had vanished inside a white billowing cloud appearing as if from nowhere.

AUTHOR'S NOTES

While *Charlie's Ashes* is a work of fiction, the author counted the Crispy Warrior WWII characters in the story as the dearest of friends, having breakfasted with them weekly, visioned the story with them, and interviewed them to learn of their lives, experiences, patriotism, and extraordinary heroism.

Readers may wonder at the truth of the flashbacks in the story; whether the principal character relationships were as depicted; whether Sam Lombardo, the Italian immigrant, led his battalion across the snow-covered minefield, flew the first American flag (handmade) on German soil, and appeared at halftime at the 2020 Super Bowl in Hard Rock Stadium in Miami Gardens, Florida; whether John Beard was a young hobo and the only pilot to fly three combat tours in WWII, and could write and recite poetry with the best of laureates; whether Bill McCowen flew the most combat missions in Air Force history (697) and flew the flare mission that "saved the bacon" for the 1st Battalion, 7th Cavalry the first night of the Battle of the Ia Drang Valley, popularized in the book written by Lieutenant General Hal Moore and Joe Galloway and featured in the film, *We Were Soldiers Once … and Young*; whether Joe Gossen was foolish enough to extend his combat tour as a ball turret gunner in a B-17 in hopes of collecting on a $300 debt; whether Tommy McCraney served in a six-man Marine Recon team near the DMZ and turned his life around after battling PTSD and drugs; and whether the Crispy Warriors veterans group has as much fun and fellowship as portrayed in the story. The reader may take heart in knowing that these things and more are, to the author's knowledge, based in fact, documented history, or personal recollections.

The author and all the WWII story characters, except Bill McCowen who passed away just a month before, made a road trip from Fort Walton Beach to the WWII Museum in New Orleans on November 19-20, 2019. Also making the trip was Gretchen Erickson, Joe Gossen's daughter. An immersive and emotional time was had at the extraordinary Windsor Court Hotel, experiencing a gala banquet and night's stay, followed the next day by a viewing of the 4-D film, *Beyond all Boundaries* and a well-guided tour of the spectacular WWII Museum.

The Cast

Lieutenant Colonel Sam Lombardo (1919-2021), one month shy of 102, outlived two wives, served in WWII, Korea, and Vietnam. Born in Calabria, Italy, he immigrated at age ten to the USA, arriving at Ellis Island a week before the 1929 stock market crash. When war loomed, he enlisted in the National Guard, graduated from Officer Candidate School, and against his wish to see combat as soon as possible was retained stateside to teach map reading skills. Finally arriving at Normandy in November 1944, he was assigned as an infantry platoon leader and company executive officer. A month later he fought in the Battle of the Bulge, and later was with the first American division to enter Germany, fighting in many other engagements en route to Germany's surrender. His early life and WWII experiences are recounted in his memoir, *O'er the Land of the Free.*

Lieutenant Colonel John Beard (1918-2020), 102 ½, served in WWII, Korea, and Vietnam. Orphaned at age four and placed in an Odd Fellows Orphanage in Elkins, WV. In 1931, after finishing elementary school, he took on a self-imposed dare, hopping a train to be the first to ever run away from the orphanage … expecting to return. Caught by railroad agents, he spent three weeks in jail and was not allowed to return to the orphanage. A hobo at 13, he rode the trains until 1940 when he thought he would serve his country and get three meals a day. His answer to an Army recruiter who asked if he had a high school diploma triggered a life unparalleled in American history.

Lieutenant Colonel Bill McCowen (1926-2019), 93, served in WWII, Korea, and Vietnam. Born in near poverty and tall for his age, he was an all-star high school athlete, lettering 14 times. Enlisting at 17, he served as an aircraft gunner in Italy during WWII. After college on the GI Bill, he was commissioned in the Air Force, flying Strategic Air Command bombers (B-29, B-47, B-52), including eight years carrying six thermonuclear bombs with Moscow as his target. Answering an urgent Air Force request for experienced pilots to fly combat tours in Vietnam, he concluded his military service with 697 combat missions, arguably the most in Air Force history.

Staff Sergeant Joe Gossen (1925-2021), 96, was adopted at birth and lied about his age to enter the Army Air Corps in 1943. Trained as an aircraft gunner, he was shipped to Italy and flew 57 missions as a ball turret gunner in a B-17 Flying Fortress. Discharged after treatment for PTSD, he attended college and for 33 years worked for the Arizona Public Service, providing electricity as a lineman and later as a general foreman. But what gave him the greatest joy in life was serving 36 years as scoutmaster for his children and grandchildren.

Corporal Charlie Geiger (1925-2018), 93, served as a GI in WWII, joining the Army in June 1944 at the age of 19 and fighting in the Battle of the Bulge. During the battle, he was hospitalized for frostbite and discharged in June 1946 at the high rank of corporal. After college and law school, he worked 30 years as a banking executive and then 16 years in the international oil and gas industry, retiring as a company president.

Private Tommy (TM) McCraney, born in Alabama in 1949, dropped out of high school, traveled to California, received a Marine Corps offer he couldn't refuse. He trained for reconnaissance work and served on a Recon team in Vietnam in 1968-69. Returning to the states, he dealt with PTSD and self-medication issues. Eventually overcoming his dependencies, a failed first marriage, and a bout with stomach cancer, he found faith, turned his life around, remarried, and has served as a deacon in his church.

Colonel Ron (Igor) Webb, born 1937, was commissioned in the Air Force in 1960 and beginning in 1966 flew fifty-three F-4 Phantom combat missions before ejecting over North Vietnam on June 1, 1967, spending six years as a POW in Hanoi, the last three years in the so called "Hanoi Hilton," (Hoa Lo), in a cell containing 46 men, several becoming general/flag officers after their release in 1973, he himself serving in high profile positions with the Federal Aeronautics Administration until retiring in 1995 to volunteer, promote conservative values, and lecture on subjects military, historical, combat, and survival.

Lieutenant Colonel Westy Westenbarger, The Crispy Warrior's moderator, born 1946, entered the Air Force in 1972, and while stationed at Udorn, Thailand, 1974-75, flew 150 F-4 Phantom missions for allied units and in support of the evacuation of allied personnel from South Vietnam. He retired in 1995 and among other pursuits taught ROTC at Niceville High School for 12 years.

Master Chief Murray Casey, born 1965, served 26 years as a Navy SEAL, 1990-2016, including combat deployments as a member of Seal Teams One and Ten, participating with the initial post-9/11 invasion force into Iraq and eight deployments to Afghanistan, a total of nine special operations deployments.

Rachel Davis, waited on the Crispy Warriors eight years at Crackings in Destin, FL. During this time, she married and had three boys. Never without a smile, her affections for the group, her ability to "handle them," and her uncanny memory of what many of them wanted for breakfast, helped shape the Crispy Warrior fellowship.

The Crew at Crackings, 11/2/2017

L-R, Charlie Geiger, John Beard, Gov. Mike Huckabee, Sam Lombardo, Bill McCowen

L-R, John Beard, Gov. Huckabee, Sam Lombardo, Charlie Geiger, Bill McCowen

The Crew without Charlie Geiger and with Joe Gossen, 10/4/18

L-R, Sam Lombardo, John Beard, Bill McCowen, Joe Gossen

The Real Road Trip – November 19-20, 2019

En route to the WWII Museum.
L-R, John Beard, Gretchen Erikson, Joe Gossen,
author Richard Adams, Sam Lombardo,

WWII Museum, Road to Berlin.
L-R, Sam Lombardo, Joe Gossen, Dan Adams,
Ken Leone, John Beard.

WWII Museum, Boeing Air Pavilion.
John Beard in front of the B-25 Mitchell bomber,
the plane he flew for a record 105 combat
mission in the European and Pacific theaters.

WWII Museum, Road to Berlin.
Clint McCowen (representing his father, Bill
McCowen), Sam Lombardo, and Joe Gossen.

WWII veterans, family, and friends at the Windsor Court Hotel, 11/19/19
L-R: Joe Gossen, daughter Gretchen, John Beard, Cheryl, Mark, and Michele Lombardo,
Clint McCowen (representing Bill McCowen), Sam Lombardo, Tom and Shirley Godbold,
Dan Adams, Mary Ann and Ken Leone, and author Richard Adams.

The Crispy Warriors, 8/19/22

ABOUT THE AUTHOR
(www.RichardBarlowAdams.com)

Richard (Rich) Adams, the first of three brothers to graduate from the United States Military Academy (West Point), Vietnam veteran, Army aviator, engineer, consultant, novelist, and Crispy Warrior since 2012, maintains the Destin Crispy Warrior Directory. Happily married to Debbie since 1971, they have a daughter, a son, five grandchildren, amazing "in-laws," and are members of the Destin United Methodist Church. His life journey largely follows that of his father, Colonel Ernest C. Adams (1913-1976), U.S. Army, Corps of Engineers, who was raised a farm boy near Effingham, IL, rode a horse to high school, was the first in the family to go to college (University of Illinois), the Distinguished Graduate of his ROTC class, served as an amphibious landings expert in WWII and Korea, and was listed for promotion to brigadier general before sustaining a career-ending heart attack. Rich has also been inspired by his father-in-law, Kenneth V. Pierce (1926-2015), a citizen soldier Navy/Marine medical corpsman who served in the Pacific theater in China in WWII and then in the Korean War.

ACKNOWLEDGEMENTS

Charlie's Ashes owes its telling to the five "Greatest Generation" WWII veterans featured in the story and to the small group veterans who first met for fellowship in the late 1990s. They assembled around "the big round table" at Destin's Harbor Docks and were led by Jerry Stalnaker, who moved to Jacksonville in 2014 and formed another veteran's group.

The author wishes to thank the following for making *Charlie's Ashes* possible and offers heartfelt apologies to anyone who doesn't see their name and believes they should have.

- Members past, present, and future of the Crispy Warriors and similar U.S. veteran groups and families throughout the country (and indeed the world).
- The men, women, and families of our armed forces and first responders who safeguard our lives and liberties.
- All those in government at the national, state, and local levels who have supported and recognized our nation's veterans and first responders.
- Tommy and Marcia Greene, owners of Crackings, and their son Preston who manages the Destin restaurant—home of the Crispy Warriors.
- The wait and kitchen staff of Crackings, past, present, and future, especially Rachel Davis who has moved on and most recently Ansley Thompson who have taken such amazing care of the Crispy Warriors.
- The author's son Richie Adams (film/TV writer, director, producer) and his executive assistant Matt LaFont (editor) of River Road Creative (www.RRC.la), for filming and recording the interviews of our WWII veterans and their trip to the WWII Museum.
- The WWII Museum and the Windsor Court Hotel for making the WWII veterans trip to New Orleans so special.
- The author's brother, Dan Adams (West Point graduate, Lieutenant Colonel, Vietnam veteran, and WWII Museum

volunteer) for organizing lodging and dinner arrangements at the Windsor Court and conducting the museum tour for our WWII veterans.

- Governor Mike Huckabee, 2016 Presidential candidate, who honored our WWII veterans at a gala 2017 Crispy Warriors breakfast.

- Florida Representative, Judge, General, and Crispy Warrior Patt Maney and his wife Caroline for all they do.

- Tom Rice, First Sergeant, Vietnam veteran, patriot, and owner of the Fort Walton Beach eatery, *Magnolia Grill,* where so many good times and great food have been enjoyed by WWII veterans, Crispy Warriors, other veterans, first responders, and the community.

- Lieutenant Colonel Sam Lombardo's children Mark and Michele, and their families.

- Lieutenant Colonel Bill & Beverly McCowen's son Clint McCowan and his wife Lisa.

- Lieutenant Colonel John & Gwen Beard's daughter Kerry Meyer and her family.

- Staff Sergeant Joe Gossen's daughter Gretchen Erickson (and family) for her indispensable help with the WWII Museum trip and her leadership with the *Veterans Heritage Project.*

- Stalwart encouragers of our Crispy Warrior WWII veterans, including and but not limited to Tom & Shirley Godbold, Jeff & Terri Marken, Jeff and Debbie Carlisi, Westy & Kay Westenbarger, Ken & Mary Ann Leone, John & Sandra Cork, Murray & Lydia Casey, Larry & Kay Hines, Rick & Debbie Scali, Skip & Brenda Overdier, Roy & Janet Taylor.

Ron DeSantis, Gulf War veteran, Naval Reserve Lieutenant Commander, Florida Governor reelected to a second term, standing with Crispy Warrior Doug Stauffer, Pastor, USSC Chaplain Brigadier